1,000,0oo Books

are available to read at

---◇---

www.ForgottenBooks.com

---◇---

Read online
Download PDF
Purchase in print

ISBN 978-0-243-46058-8
PIBN 10800126

1 MONTH OF
FREE
READING

at

www.ForgottenBooks.com

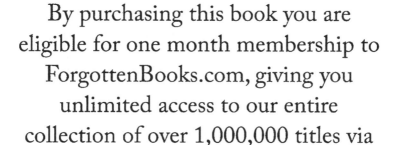

By purchasing this book you are eligible for one month membership to ForgottenBooks.com, giving you unlimited access to our entire collection of over 1,000,000 titles via our web site and mobile apps.

To claim your free month visit:

www.forgottenbooks.com/free800126

English
Français
Deutsche
Italiano
Español
Português

www.forgottenbooks.com

Mythology Photography **Fiction**
Fishing Christianity **Art** Cooking
Essays Buddhism Freemasonry
Medicine **Biology** Music **Ancient**
Egypt Evolution Carpentry Physics
Dance Geology **Mathematics** Fitness
Shakespeare **Folklore** Yoga Marketing
Confidence Immortality Biographies
Poetry **Psychology** Witchcraft
Electronics Chemistry History **Law**
Accounting **Philosophy** Anthropology
Alchemy Drama Quantum Mechanics
Atheism Sexual Health **Ancient History**
Entrepreneurship Languages Sport
Paleontology Needlework Islam
Metaphysics Investment Archaeology
Parenting Statistics Criminology
Motivational

E and YARICO:

A N

P E R A.

ice One Shilling and Sixpence.

INKLE and YARICO:

AN

OPERA.

IN THREE ACTS,

AS PERFORMED AT THE

THEATRE-ROYAL

IN THE

HAY-MARKET.

First Acted on Saturday, August 11th, 1787.

***

WRITTEN BY

GEORGE COLMAN, Junior.

***

SECOND EDITION.

***

LONDON:

DRAMATIS PERSONÆ.

Inkle,	-	- Mr. BANNISTER, Jun.
Sir Chriſtopher Curry,		- Mr. PARSONS.
Medium,	-	- Mr. BADDELEY.
Campley,	-	- Mr. DAVIES.
Trudge,	-	- Mr. EDWIN.
Mate,	-	- Mr. MÉADOWS.

Planters, Sailors, &c.

WOMEN.

Yarico,	-	- Mrs. KEMBLE.
Narciſſa,	-	- Mrs. BANNISTER.
Wowſki,	-	- Miſs GEORGE.
Patty,	-	- Mrs. FORSTER.

SCENE———*Firſt on the Main of* America : *Afterwards in* Barbadoes.

(The Lines in inverted Commas are omitted in Repreſentation.)

INKLE and YARICO:

AN

OPERA.

ACT. I.

SCENE I.

An American *Foreſt.*

Medium (without). HILLI ho! ho!
Trudge (without). Hip! hollo! ho! ho!---Hip!---

Enter Medim *and* Trudge.

Med. Pſhaw! it's only waſting time and breath. Bawling won't perſuade him to budge a bit faſter. Things are all alter'd now; and, whatever weight it may have in *ſome* places, bawling, it ſeems, don't go for argument, here. Plague on't! we are now in the wilds of America.

Trudge. Hip, hillio---ho---hi!---

Med. Hold your tongue, you blockhead, or---

Trudge. Lord! Sir, if my maſter makes no more haſte, we ſhall all be put to ſword by the knives of the natives. I'm told they take off heads like hats, and hang 'em on pegs in their parlours. Mercy on us! My head

aches

aches with the very thoughts of it. Holo! Mr. Inkle! mafter; holo!

Med. Head aches! Zounds, fo does mine with your confounded bawling. It's enough to bring all the natives about us; and we fhall be ftript and plunder'd in a minute.

Trudge. Aye; ftripping is the firft thing that would happen to us; for they feem to be woefully off for a wardrobe. I myfelf faw three at a diftance with lefs cloaths than I have when I get out of bed; all dancing about in black buff; juft like Adam in mourning.

Med. This it is to have to do with a fchemer! a fellow who rifques his life, for a chance of advancing his intereft.---Always advantage in view! Trying, here, to make difcoveries that may promote his profit in England. Another Botany Bay fcheme, mayhap. Nothing elfe could induce him to quit our foraging party, from the fhip; when he knows every inhabitant here is not only as black as a pepper-corn, but as hot into the bargain--- and *I*, like a fool, to follow him! and then to let him loiter behind.---Why, Nephew!--Why, Inkle.--(*calling.*)

Trudge. Why, Inkle---Well! only to fee the difference of men! he'd have thought it very hard, now, if I had let him call fo often after me. Ah! I wifh he was calling after me now, in the old jog-trot way, again. What a fool was I to leave London for foreign parts! ---That ever I fhou'd leave Threadneedle-ftreet, to thread an American foreft, where a man's as foon loft as a needle in a bottle of hay.

Med. Patience, Trudge! Patience! If we once recover the fhip———.

Trudge. Lord, fir, I fhall never recover what I have loft in coming abroad. When my mafter and I were in London, I had fuch a mortal fnug birth of it! Why I was *factotum.*

Med. Factotum to a young merchant is no fuch finecure, neither.

Trudge. But then the honor of it. Think of that, fir; to be clerk as well as *own man.* Only confider. You find very few city clerks made out of a man, now-
a-days.

a-days. To be king of the counting-houfe, as well as lo:d of the bed-chamber. Ah! if I had him but now in the little dreffing-room behind the office; tying his hair, with a bit of red tape as ufual.

Med. Yes, or writing an invoice in lampblack, and fhining his fhoes-with an ink bottle *as ufual,* you blundering blockhead!

Trudge. Oh if I was but brufhing the accounts, or cafting up the coats! mercy on us! What's that?

Med. That! What?

Trudge. Didn't you hear a noife?

Med. Y---es--but---hufh! Oh heaven be prais'd, here he is at laft.

Enter Inkle.

Now nephew!

Inkle. So, Mr Medium.

Med. Zounds, one wou'd think, by your confounded compofure, that you were walking in St. James's Park inftead of an American foreft: and that all the beafts were nothing but good company. The hollow trees here, centry boxes, and the lions in 'em foldiers; the jackalls, courtiers; the crocodiles, fine women; and the baboons, beaux. What the plague made you loiter fo long?

Inkle. Reflection.

Med. So I fhould think; reflection generally comes lagging behind. What, fcheming, I fuppofe? never quiet. At it again, eh? What a happy trader is your father, to have fo prudent a fon for a partner! Why, you are the carefulleft Co. in the whole city. Never lofing fight of the main chance; and that's the reafon, perhaps, you loft fight of us, here, on the main of America.

Innle. Right, Mr. Medium. Arithmetic, I own, has been the means of our parting at prefent.

Trudge. Ha! A fum in divifion I reckon. (*Afide*)

Med. And pray, if I may be fo bold, what mighty fcheme has juft tempted you to employ your head, when you ought to make ufe of your heels?

Inkle. My heels! Here's pretty doctrine! Do you think I travel merely for motion? A fine expenfive plan

for

for a trader truly.   What, wou'd you have a man of
bufinefs come abroad, fcamper extravagantly here and
there and every where, then return home, and have
nothing to tell, but that he has *been* here and there and
every where?   'Sdeath, Sir, would you have me travel
like a lord?

Med.   No, the Lord forbid! "but I am wrong
"perhaps! there is fomething in the air of this foreft,
"I believe, that inclines people to be hafty."

Inkle.   Travelling, Uncle, was always intended for
improvement; and improvement is an advantage; and
advantage is profit, and profit is gain.   Which, in the
travelling tranflation of a trader, means, that you fhou'd
gain every advantage of improving your profit.

"*Med.*   How---gain, and advantage, and profit?
"Zounds I'm quite at a lofs."

"*Inkle.*   You've hit it, Uncle! fo am I.   I have loft
"my clue by your converfation: you have knock'd all
"my meditations on the head."

"*Med.*   Its very lucky for you no-body has done it
"before me."

Inkle.   I have been comparing the land, here, with
that of our own country.

Med.   And you find it like a good deal of the land of
our own country---curfedly encumber'd with black legs,
I take it.

Inkle.   And calculating how much it might be made
to produce by the acre.

Med.   You were?

Inkle.   Yes, I was proceeding algebraically upon the
fubject.

Med.   Indeed!

Inkle.   And juft about extracting the fquare root.

Med.   Hum!

Inkle.   I was thinking too, if fo many natives cou'd
be caught, how much they might fetch at the Weft India
markets.

Med.   Now let me afk you a queftion, or two, young
Cannibal Catcher, if you pleafe.

Inkle.   Well.

Med.

Med. Arn't we bound for Barbadoes, partly to trade, but chiefly to carry home the daughter of the governor, Sir Chriftopher Curry, who has till now been under your father's care, in Threadneedle-ftreet, for polite Englifh education?

Inkle. Granted.

Med. And isn't it determin'd, between the old folks, that you are to marry Narciffa as foon as we get there?

Inkle. A fix'd thing.

Med. Then what the devil do you do here, hunting old hairy negroes, when you ought to be ogling a fine girl in the ship? Algebra too! You'll have other things to think of when you are married, I promife you! a plodding fellow's head, in the hands of a young wife, like a boy's flate after fchool, foon gets all its arithmetick wip'd off: and then it appears in its true fimple ftate: dark, empty, and bound in wood, Mafter Inkle.

Inkle. Not in a match of this kind. Why it's a table of intereft from beginning to end, old Medium.

Med. Well, well, this is no time to talk. Who knows but, inftead of failing to a wedding, we may get cut up here for a wedding dinner: tofs'd up for a dingy duke perhaps, or ftew'd down for a black baronet, or eat raw by an Inky commoner.

Inkle. Why fure you arn't afraid?

Med. Who, I afraid! Ha! ha! ha! No, not I! What the deuce fhould I be afraid of? Thank heaven I have a clear confcience, and need not be afraid of any thing. A fcoundrel might not be quite fo eafy on fuch an occafion; but it's the part of an honeft man not to behave like a fcoundrel. I never behav'd like a fcoundrel---for which reafon I am an honeft man you know. But come---I hate to boaft of my good qualities.

Inkle. Slow and fure, my good virtuous Mr. Medium! Our companions can be but half a mile before us: and if we do but double their fteps, we fhall overtake 'em at one mile's end, by all the powers of arithmetick.

B 2

Med.

Med. Oh curfe your arithmetick! How are we to find our way?

Inkle. That, Uncle, muft be left to the doctrine of chances. [*Exeunt.*

SCENE, *another part of the Forest.*

A fhip at anchor in the bay at a fmall diftance.

Enter Sailors *and* Mate, *as returning from for-*
aging.

Mate Come, come, bear a hand, my lads. Tho'f the bay is juft under our bowfprits, it will take a damn'd deal of tripping to come at it---there's hardly any fteering clear of the rocks here. But do we mufter all hands? All right, think ye?

" *Sailors.* All, all, my hearty."

" *Mate.* What Nick Noggin---Ralph Reef---Tom
" Pipes---Jack Rattlin---Dick Deck---Mat Maft---
" Sam Surf---Ten water cafks, and a hog?"

1*ft Sail.* All to a man---befides yourfelf, and a monkey---the three land lubbers, that edg'd away in the morning, goes for nothing you know---they're all dead may hap by this.

Mate. Dead! you be---Why they're friends of the Captain; and if not brought fafe aboard to-night, you may all chance to have a falt eel for your fupper---that's all.---Moreover the young plodding fpark, he with the grave, foul weather face there, is to man the tight little frigate, Mifs Narciffa, what d'ye call her, that is bound with us for Barbadoes. Rot 'em for not keeping under way, I fay.

" 2*d Sail.* Foolifh dogs! Suppofe they are met by
" the Natives."

Mate. " Why then the Natives would look plaguy
" black upon 'em, I do fuppofe." But come, let's fee if a fong will bring 'em to. Let's have a full chorus to the good Merchant Ship the Achilles, that's wrote by our Captain. " Where's Tom Pipes?"

" *Sail.*

Sails. Here!*

"*Mate.* Come then, Pipe all hands. Crack the drums
" of their ears, my tight fellow. Hail 'em with your
" singing trumpet."

S O N G.

The A*c*hilles, though christen'd, good ship, 'tis surmis'd,
From that old Man of War, great A*c*hilles, so priz'd,
Was he, like our vessel, pray, fairly baptized?
Ti tol lol, &c.

II.

Poets sung that *Achilles* ---if, now, they've an itch
To sing this, future ages may know which is which;
And that one rode in Greece---and the other in Pitch.
Ti tol lol, &c.

III.

What tho' but a Merchant ship---sure our supplies:
Now your Men of War's gain in a lottery lies,
And how blank they all look, when they can't get a prize!
Ti tol lol, &c.

IV.

What are all their fine names? when no Rhino's behind,
The Intrepid, and Lion, look sheepish you'll find;
Whilst, alas! the poor Æolus can't raise the wind!
Ti tol lol, &c.

V.

Then the Thunderer's dumb; out of tune the Orpheus;
The Ceres has nothing at all to produce;
And the Eagle, I warrant you, looks like a goose.
Ti tol lol, &c.

VI.

But we merchant lads, tho' the foe we can't maul,
Nor are paid, like fine king-ships, to fight at a call,
Why we pay ourselves well, without fighting at all.
Ti tol lol, &c.

1st Sail. Avaſt! look a head there. Here they come chas'd by a fleet of black devils.

Midſh. And the devil a *fire* have I to give 'em. We han't a grain of Powder left. What muſt we do, lads?

2d Sail. Do? Sheer off to be ſure.

" *Midſh.* What, and leave our companions behind?"

" *1ſt Sail.* Why not? they left us before; ſo it " comes to the ſame thing.

" *Midſh.* No damn it—I can't---I can't do that " neither."

" *3d Sail.* Why then we'll leave you. Who the " plague is to ſtand here, and be peppered by a parcel " of ſavages?

" *Midſh.* Why to be ſure as it is ſo---plague on't " (*reluctantly*).

" *1ſt Sail.* Paw mun, they're as ſafe as we. Why " we're ſcarce a cable's length aſunder; and they'll keep " in our wake, now, I warrant 'em.

" *Midſh.* Why, if you will have it ſo---It makes a " body's heart yearn to leave the poor fellows in diſtreſs, " too."

All. Come bear a hand, Maſter Malinſpike.

Midſh. (*Reluctantly*). Well if I muſt, I muſt (*going to the other ſide and hallowing to* Inkle, &c.) Yoho, Lubbers! Crowd all the ſail you can, dye mind me?

[*Exeunt Sailors.*

Enter Medium, *running acroſs the ſtage as purſued by the Blacks.*

Med. Nephew! Trudge! run---ſcamper! Scour--- fly! Zounds, what harm did I ever do to be hunted to death by a pack of black bloodhounds? Why Nephew! O confound your long ſums in arithmetick! I'll take care of myſelf; and if we muſt have any arithmetick, dot and carry one for my money. (*runs off.*)

Enter Inkle *and* Trudge *haſtily.*

Trudge. Oh! that ever I was born, to leave pen, ink, and powder for this!

Inkle.

Inkle. Trudge, how far are the failors before us?

Trudge. I'll run and fee, Sir, directly.

Inkle. Blockhead, come here. The favages are clofe upon us; we fhall fcarce be able to recover our party. Get behind this tuft of trees with me; they'll pafs us, and we may then recover the fhip with fafety.

Trudge. (*going behind*) Oh! Threadneedle-ftreet, Thread!——

Inkle. Peace.

Trudge. (*hiding*)---Needle-ftreet. (*They hide behind trees. Natives crofs. After a long paufe,* Inkle *looks from the trees.*

Inkle. Trudge.

Trudge. Sir. (*In a whifper*).

Inkle. Are they all gone by?

Trudge. Won't you look and fee?

Inkle. (*Looking round*). So, all's fafe at laft. (*coming forward.*) Nothing like policy in thefe cafes; but you'd have run on like a booby! A tree, I fancy, you'll find, in future, the beft refource in a hot purfuit.

Trudge. Oh charming! It's a retreat for a king, Sir. Mr. Medium, however, has not got up in it; your Uncle, Sir, has *run on like a booby*; and has got up with our party by this time, I take it; who are now moft likely at the fhore. But what are we to do next, Sir?

Inkle. Reconnoitre a little, and then proceed.

Trudge. Then pray, Sir, proceed to reconnoitre; for the fooner the better.

Inkle. Then look out, d'ye hear, and tell me, if you difcover any danger.

Trudge. Y--- Ye---s---Yes. But (*trembling*). " As you underftand this bufinefs better than I, Sir, fup- " pofe you ftick clofe to my elbow to give me direc- " tions.

" *Inkle.* Cowardly fcoundrel! Do as you are order'd, " Sir." Well, is the coaft clear?

Trudge. Eh! Oh Lord!---Clear? (*rubbing his eyes*) Oh dear! oh dear! the coaft will foon be clear enough now, I promife you——The fhip is under fail, Sir.

Inkle.

" *Inkle.* Death and damnation !

" *Trudge.* Aye, death falls to *my* lot. I fhall ftarve
" and go off like a pop-gun."

Inkle. Confufion ! my property carried off in the
veffel.

Trudge. All, all, Sir, except me.

" *Inkle.* Treacherous villains ! My whole effects
" loft.

Trudge. Lord, Sir, any body but you wou'd only
" think of effecting his fafety in fuch a fituation."

Inkle. They may report me dead, perhaps, and dif-
pofe of my property at the next ifland.

(*The veffel appears under fail.*)

Trudge. Ah ! there they go. (*A gun fir'd.*)
That will be the laft report we fhall ever hear from 'em,
I'm afraid.---That's as much as to fay, Good bye to ye.
And here we are left---two fine, full-grown babes in the
wood !

Inkle. What an ill-tim'd accident ! Juft too, when
my fpeedy union with Narciffa, at Barbadoes, wou'd fo
much advance my interefts. Something muft be hit upon, and fpeedily ; but what refource ! (*thinkiug.*)

Trudge. The old one---a tree, Sir,---It's all we
have for it now. What wou'd I give now, to be perch'd
upon a high ftool, with our brown defk fqueez'd into
the pit of my ftomach---fcribbling away on an old parch-
ment !---But all my red ink will be fpilt by an old black
pin of a negro.

SONG.

Laft Valentine's Day.

A voyage over feas had not enter'd my head,
Had I known but on which fide to butter my bread,
Heigho ! fure I---for hunger muft die !
I've fail'd like a booby ; come here in a fquall,
Where, alas ! there's no bread to be butter'd at all !
Oho ! I'm a terrible booby !
Oh, what a fad booby am I !

II.

In London, what gay chop-house signs in the street!
But the only sign here is of nothing to eat.
Heigho! that I---for hunger shou'd die!
My mutton's all lost; I'm a poor starving elf;
And for all the world like a lost mutton myself.
Oho! I shall die a lost mutton!
Oh what a lost mutton am I!

III.

For a neat slice of beef, I could roar like a bull;
And my stomach's so empty, my heart is quite full.
Heigho! that I---for hunger should die!
But, grave without meat, I must here meet my grave,
For my bacon, I fancy, I never shall save.
Oho! I shall ne'er save my bacon!
I can't save my bacon, not I!

Trudge. Hum! I was thinking————

" *Inkle.* Well, well, what? Something to our purpose, I hope.

Trudge. I was thinking, Sir,---if so many natives cou'd be caught, how much they might fetch at the West India markets!

Inkle. Scoundrel! is this a time to jest?

Trudge. No, faith, Sir! Hunger is too sharp to be jested with. As for me, I shall starve for want of food. Now you may meet a luckier fate: You are able to extract the square root, Sir; and that's the very best provision you can find here to live upon. But I! *(noise at a distance.)* Mercy on us! here they come again.

Inkle. Confusion! Deserted on one side, and press'd on the other, which way shall I turn?---This cavern may prove a safe retreat to us for the present. I'll enter, cost what it will.

Trudge. Oh Lord! no, don't, don't---We shall pay too dear for our lodging, depend on't.

Inkle. This is no time for debating. You are at the mouth of it; lead the way, Trudge.

C

Trudge.

Trudge. What! go in before your honor! I know my place better, I assure you.---I might walk into more mouths than one, perhaps. *(Aside)*

Inkle. Coward! then follow me. *(Noise again.)*

Trudge. I must, Sir; I must! Ah Trudge, Trudge! what a damn'd hole are you getting into!

[*Exeunt into a cavern.*

SCENE, *A Cave, decorated with skins of wild beasts, feathers, &c. in the middle of the scene, a rude kind of curtain, by way of door to an apartment.*

Enter Inkle *and* Trudge, *as from the mouth of the Cavern.*

Trudge. Why, Sir! Sir! you must be mad to go any farther.

Inkle. So far, at least, we have proceeded with safety. Ha! no bad specimen of savage elegance. These ornaments wou'd be worth something in England.---We have little to fear here, I hope: This cave rather bears the pleasing face of a profitable adventure.

Trudge. Very likely, Sir! But for a pleasing face, it has the cursed'st ugly mouth I ever saw in my life. Now do, Sir, make off as fast as you can. If we once get clear of the natives houses, we have little to fear from the lions and leopards: for, by the appearance of their parlours, they seem to have kill'd all the wild beasts in the country. Now pray, do, my good Master, take my advice, and run away.

Inkle. Rascal! Talk again of going out, and I'll flea you alive.

Trudge. That's just what I expect for coming in.--- All that enter here appear to have had their skin stript over their ears; and ours will be kept for curiosities---. We shall stand, here, stuff'd, for a couple of white wonders.

Inkle. This curtain seems to lead to another apartment: I'll draw it.

Trudge.

Trudge. No, no, no, don't; don't. We may be call'd to account for difturbing the company: you may get a curtain-lecture, perhaps, Sir.

Inkle. Peace, booby, and ftand on your guard.

Trudge. Oh! what will become of us! Some grim, feven foot fellow ready to fcalp us.

Inkle. By heaven! a woman.

As the curtain draws, Yarico *and* Wowfki *difcover'd afleep.*

Trudge. A woman! (*Afide.*) (*Loud.*) But let him come on; I'm ready—dam'me, I don't fear facing the devil himfelf.----Faith it is a woman---faft afleep, too.

Inkle. And beautiful as an angel!

Trudge. And, egad! there feems to be a nice little plump bit in the corner; only fhe's an angel of rather a darker fort.

Inkle. Hufh! keep back---fhe wakes. [Yarico *comes forward---*Inkle *and* Trudge *retire to oppofite fides of the fcene.*]

SONG.——YARICO.

When the chace of day is done,
And the fhaggy lion's fkin,
Which for us our warriors win,
Decks our cell at fet of fun;
Worn with toil, with fleep oppreft,
I prefs my moffy bed, and fink to reft.

II.

Then, once more, I fee our train,
With all our chace renew'd again:
Once more 'tis day,
Once more our prey
Gnafhes his angry teeth, and foams in vain.
Again, in fullen hafte, he flies,
Ta'en in the toil, again he lies,
Again he roars, and in my flumbers dies.

C 2

Inkle.

Inkle. Our language!

Trudge. Zounds, she has thrown me into a cold sweat.

Yarico. Hark! I heard a noise! Wowski, awake! whence can it proceed! [*She wakes Wowski, and they both come forward---Yarico towards Inkle; Wowski towards* Trudge.]

" *Trudge.* Madam, your very humble servant."
[*to Wowski*]

Yar. Ah! what form is this?---are you a man?

Inkle. True flesh and blood, my charming heathen, I promise you.

Yar. What harmony in his voice! What a shape! How fair his skin too!------(*gazing.*)

Trudge. This must be a lady of quality, by her staring.

Yar. Say, stranger, whence come you?------

Inkle. From a far distant island; driven on this coast by distress, and deserted by my companions.

Yar. And do you know the danger that surrounds you here? Our woods are fill'd with beasts of prey---my countrymen too---(Yet, I think they cou'd n't find the heart)---might kill you.---It wou'd be a pity if you fell in their way---I think I shou'd weep if you came to any harm.

Trudge. O ho! It's time I see to begin making interest with the chambermaid. (*Takes* Wowski *apart.*)

Inkle. How wild and beautiful! sure there's magic in her shape, and she has rivetted me to the place; but where shall I look for safety? let me fly, and avoid my death.

Yarico. Oh! no, but---(*as if puzzled*) well then, die stranger, but don't depart.---But I will try to preserve you; and if you are kill'd, Yarico must die too! Yet, 'tis I alone can save you: your death is certain without my assistance; and indeed, indeed, you shall shall not want it.

Inkle. My kind Yarico! but what means must be us'd for my safety?

Yarico. My cave must conceal you: none enter it since my father was slain in battle. I will bring you food

by

by day, then lead you to our unfrequented groves by
moonlight, to liſten to the nightingale. If you ſhould
ſleep, I'll watch you, and wake you when there's danger.

Inkle. Generous Maid! Then, to you I will owe my
life; and whilſt it laſts, nothing ſhall part us.

Yar. And ſhan't it, ſhan't it indeed?

Inkle. No, my Yarico! For when an opportunity
offers to return to my country, you ſhall be my Companion.

Yar. What, croſs the ſeas?

Inkle. Yes, help me to diſcover a veſſel, and you ſhall
enjoy wonders. You ſhall be deck'd in ſilks, my brave
maid, and have a houſe drawn with horſes to carry you.

Yar. Nay, do not laugh at me---but is it ſo?

Inkle. It is indeed!

Yar. Oh wonder! I wiſh my countrywomen cou'd
ſee me———But won't your warriors kill us?

Inkle. No, our only danger on land is here.

Yar. Then let us retire further into the cave. Come
---your ſafety is in my keeping.

Inkle. I follow you---Yet, can you run ſome riſque
in following me?

D U E T T.

O ſay, Bonny Laſs.

Inkle. *O ſay, ſimple maid, have you form'd any notion*
Of all the rude dangers in croſſing the ocean?
When winds whiſtle ſhrilly, ah! won't they re-
mind you,
To ſigh with regret for the grot left behind you?

Yar. *Ah! no, I cou'd follow, and ſail the world over,*
Nor think of my grot, when I look at my lover!
The winds which blow round us, your arms for
my pillow,
Will lull us to ſleep, whilſt we're rock'd by each
billow.

Inkle. *Then, ſay, lovely laſs, what if haply eſpying*
A rich gallant veſſel with gay colours flying?

" Yar. *I'll journey, with thee, love, to where the land*
      narrows,
    " *And fling all my cares at my back with my*
      arrows."

Both. *O say then, my true love, we never will sunder,*
    Nor shrink from the tempest, nor dread the big
      thunder :
    Whilst constant, we'll laugh at all changes of
      weather,
    And journey, all over the world, both together.
    [Exeunt as retiring further into the Cave]

Manent Trudge *and* Wowski.

Trudge. Why you speak English as well as I, my little Wowski.

Wowski. Ifs.

Trudge. Ifs ! And you learnt it from a strange man, that tumbled from a big boat, many moons ago, you say ?

Wowf. Ifs.---Teach me---Teach good many.

Trudge. Then, what the devil made 'em so surpris'd at seeing us ! was he like me ?

Wowf. (*Shakes her head.*)

Trudge. Not so smart a body may-hap. Was his face, now round, and comely; and--eh ! (*Stroaking his chin.*) Was it like mine ?

Wowf. Like dead leaf---brown and shrivel.

Trudge, Oh, oh, an old shipwreck'd sailor, I warrant; with white and grey hair, eh, my pretty beauty spot ?

Wowf. Ifs ; all white. When night come, he put it in pocket.

Trudge, Oh ! wore a wig. But the old boy taught you something more than English, I believe.

Wowf. Ifs.

Trudge. The devil he did ! What was it ?

Wowf. Teach me put dry grafs, red hot, in hollow white stick.

Trudge. Aye, what was that for ?

Wowf.

Wowf. Put in my mouth—go poff, poff?

Trudge. Zounds! did he teach you to smoke?

Wowf. Ifs.

Trudge. And what became of him at laft? What did your countrymen do for the poor fellow?

Wowf. Eat him one day---Our chief kill him.

Trudge. Mercy on us! what damn'd ftomachs, to fwallow a tough old Tar! Though for the matter of that, there's many of our Captains would eat all they kill I believe! Ah poor Trudge! your killing comes next.

Wowf. No, no---not you---no---*(running to him anxioufly)*

Trudge. No? why what fhall I do if I get in their paws?

Wowf. I fight for you!

Trudge. Will you? Ecod fhe's a brave, good-natur'd wench! fhe'll be worth a hundred of your Englifh wives--Whenever they fight on their hufband's account, it's with him inftead of for him, I fancy. But how the plague am I to live here?

Wowf. I feed you---bring you kid.

S O N G.

(One day, I heard Mary fay.)

White man, never go away—
  Tell me why need you?
Stay, with your Wowfki, *ftay:*
  Wowfki *will feed you.*
Cold moons are now coming in:
  Ah don't go grieve me!
I'll wrap you in leopard's fkin:
  White man, don't leave me.

3   II. *And*

II.

And when all the sky is blue,
Sun makes warm weather,
I'll catch you a Cockatoo,
Dress you in feather.
When cold comes, or when 'tis hot,
Ah don't go grieve me!
Poor Wowski will be forgot---
White man, don't leave me.

Trudge. Zounds! leopard's skin for winter wear, and feathers for a summer's suit!.. Ha, ha! I shall look like a walking hammer-cloth, at Christmas, and an upright shuttlecock, in the dog-days. And, for all this, if my master and I find our way to England, you shall be part of our travelling equipage; and when I get there, I'll give you a couple of snug rooms on a first floor, and visit you every evening as soon as I come from the counting house. Do you like it?

Wowf. Iss.

Trudge. Damme, what a flashy fellow I shall seem in the city! I'll get her a *white* boy to bring up the teakettle: then I'll teach you to write and dress hair.

Wowf. You great man in your country?

Trudge. Oh yes, a very great man. I'm head clerk of the counting-house, and first valet-de-chambre of the dressing-room. I pounce parchments, powder hair, black shoes, ink paper, shave beards, and mend pens. But hold; I had forgot one material point---you ar'n't married, I hope?

Wowf. No: you be my chum-chum!

Trudge. So I will. It's best, however, to be sure of her being single; for Indian husbands are not quite so complaisant as English ones, and the vulgar dogs might think of looking a little after their spouses. Well, as my master seems king of this palace, and has taken his Indian Queen already, I'll e'en be Usher of the black rod here. But you have had a lover or two in your time; eh, Wowski?

Wowf. Oh iss, great many, I tell you.

DUETT.

D U E T T.

Wowf. *Wampum, Swampum, Yanko, Lanko, Nanko,*
    Pownatowfki,
    Black men——plenty——twenty——fight for me.
    White man, woo you true?

Trudge. *Who?*
Wowf.   *You.*
Trudge.   *Yes, pretty little Wowfki!*
Wowf. *Then I leave all, and I follow thee.*
Trudge. *Oh then turn about, my little tawny tight one!*
    Don't you like me?
Wowf. *Ifs, you're like the fnow!*
    If you flight one.——
Trudge. *Never, not for any white one:*
    You are beautiful as any floe.
Wowf. *Wars, jars, fcars, can't expofe ye*
    In our grot.——
Trudge.   *So fnug and cofey!*
Wowf. *Flowers neatly*
    Pick'd, fhall fweetly
      Make your bed.
Trudge. *Coying, toying*
    With a rofy
      Pofey,
        When I'm dozey,
    Bear-fkin night-caps too fhall warm my head.
Both.   Bear-fkin night-caps, &c. &c.

End of the FIRST ACT.

ACT

ACT II.

S C E N E, *The Quay at* Barbadoes, *with an Inn upon it. People employed in unlading Veſſels, carrying Bales of Goods, &c.*

Enter ſeveral Planters.

1ſt Plant. I Saw her this morning, gentlemen, you may depend on't. My telescope never fails me. I popp'd upon her as I was taking a peep from my balcony. A brave tight ſhip, I tell you, bearing down directly for Barbadoes here.—

2d Plant. Ods my life! rare news! We have not had a veſſel arrive in our harbour theſe ſix weeks.

3d Plant. And the laſt brought only madam Narciſſa, our Governor's daughter, from England; with a parcel of lazy, idle, white folks about her. Such cargoes will never do for our Trade, neighbour.

4th Plant. No, no: we want ſlaves. A terrible dearth of 'em in Barbadoes lately! But your dingy paſſengers for my money. Give me a veſſel like a collier, where all the lading tumbles out as black as my hat. But are you ſure now you ar'n't miſtaken? *(to 1ſt Planter)*

1ſt Plant. Miſtaken! 'ſbud, do you doubt my glaſs? I can diſcover a gull by it ſix leagues off: I could ſee every thing as plain as if I was on board.

2d Plant. Indeed! and what were her colours?

1ſt Plant. Um! why Engliſh——or Dutch——or French—— I don't exactly remember.

3d Plant. What were the ſailors aboard?

1ſt Plant. Eh! why they were Engliſh too——or Dutch——or French——I can't perfectly recollect.

3

4th Plant.

4th Plant. Your glaſs, neighbour, is a little like a glaſs too much: it makes you forget every thing you ought to remember. *(Cry without,* " *A ſail, a ſail!"*

1ſt Plant. Egad but I'm right tho'. Now, gentlemen!

All. Aye, ayé; the devil take the hindmoſt.

[*Exeunt haſtily.*

Enter Narciſſa *and* Patty.

SONG.

Freſhly now the breeze is blowing;
As yon ſhip at anchor rides,
Sullen waves, inceſſant flowing,
Rudely daſh againſt the ſides:
So my heart, its courſe impeded,
Beats in my perturbed breaſt;
Doubts, like waves by waves ſucceeded,
Riſe, and ſtill deny it reſt.

Patty. Well, Ma'am, as I was ſaying————

Nar. Well, ſay no more of what you were ſaying——Sure, Patty, you forget where you are: a little caution will be neceſſary now, I think.

Patty. Lord, Madam, how is it poſſible to help talking? We are in Barbadoes here to be ſure———but then, Ma'am, one may let out a little in a private morning's walk by ourſelves.

Nar. Nay, it's the ſame thing with you in doors.

" *Patty.* Why, to ſay the truth, Ma'am, tho' we do
" live in your father's houſe—Sir Chriſtopher Curry,
" the grand Governor that governs all Barbadoes——
" and a terrible poſitive governor he is to be ſure—
" yet, he'll find it a difficult matter to govern a cham-
" bermaid's tongue, I believe.

" *Nar.* That I am ſure of, Patty; for it runs as ra-
" pidly as the tide which brought us from England.

" *Patty.* Very true, Ma'am; and like the tide it
" ſtops for no man.

D 2 *Nar.*

Women talk too much?

Female vanity

"*Nar.* Well, well, let it run as you please; only for
" my sake, take care it don't run away with you.
  "*Patty.* Oh, Ma'am, it has been too well train'd
" in the course of conversation, I promise you; and if
" ever it says any thing to your disadvantage, my name
" is not Patty Prink."---I never blab, Ma'am, never,
as I hope for a gown.

Nar. And your never blabbing, as you call it, de-
pends chiefly on that hope, I believe. The unlocking
my chest, locks up all your faculties. An old silk gown
makes you turn your back on all my secrets; a large
bonnet-blinds your eyes, and a fashionable high hand-
kerchief covers your ears, and stops your mouth at once,
Patty.

Patty. Dear Ma'am, how can you think a body so
mercenary! Am I always teasing you about gowns and
gew-gaws, and fallals and finery? Or do you take me
for a conjuror, that nothing will come out of my mouth
but ribbons? I have told the story of our voyage, indeed, to old Guzzle, the butler, who is very inquisitive;
and, between ourselves, is the ugliest old Quiz I ever saw
in my life.

Nar. Well, well, I have seen him; pitted with the
small-pox and a red face.

Patty. Right, Ma'am. It's for all the world like his
master's cellar, full of holes and liquor. But when he asks
me what you and I think of the matter, why I look wise,
and cry like other wise people who have nothing to say---
All's for the best.

Nar. And, thus, you lead him to imagine I am but
little inclin'd to the match.

Patty. Lord, Ma'am, how cou'd that be? Why, I
never said a word about Captain Campley.

Nar. Hush! hush, for heaven's sake.

Patty. Ay! there it is now.---There, Ma'am, I'm
as mute as a mack'rel---That name strikes me dumb in
a moment. I don't know how it is, but Captain Campley somehow or other has the knack of stopping my
mouth oftner than any body else, Ma'am.

Nar. His name again!---Consider.---Never mention it, I desire you.

Patty.

Patty. Not I, Ma'am, not I. But if our voyage from England was so pleasant, it wasn't owing to Mr. Inkle, I'm certain. He didn't play the fiddle in our cabin, and dance on the deck, and come languishing with a glass of warm water in his hand, when we were sea-sick. Ah, Ma'am, that water warm'd your heart, I'm confident. Mr. Inkle! No, no; Captain Cam——"there, he "has stopped my Mouth again Ma'am."

Nar. There is no end to this! Remember, Patty, keep your secrecy, or you entirely lose my favour.

Patty. Never fear me, Ma'am. But if somebody I know is not acquainted with the Governor, there's such a thing as dancing at balls, and squeezing hands when you lead up, and squeezing them again when you cast down, and walking on the Quay in a morning.

"*Nar.* No more of this!"

Patty. O, I won't utter a syllable. "I'll go, and "take a turn on the Quay by myself, if you think pro-per." (*archly*)——But remember, I'm as close as a patch-box. Mum's the word, Ma'am, I promise you.

S O N G.

This maxim let ev'ry one hear,
  Proclaim'd from the north to the south;
Whatever comes in at your ear,
  Should never run out at your mouth.
We servants, like servants of state,
  Should listen to all, and be dumb;
Let others harangue and debate,
  We look wise---shake our heads---and are mum.

II.

The Judge in dull dignity drest,
  In silence hears barristers preach;
And then, to prove silence is best,
  He'll get up, and give them a speech.

By

By saying but little, the maid
  Will keep her swain under her thumb;
And the lover, that's true to his trade,
  Is certain to kiss, and cry mum.   *[Exit.*

Nar. " This heedless wench, every time she speaks,
I dread a discovery of my sentiments." How awkward
is my present situation ! Promis'd to one, who, perhaps,
may never again be heard of; and who, I am sure, if he
ever appears to claim me, will do it merely on the score
of interest---press'd too, by another, who has already,
I fear, too much interest in my heart——what can I do?
What plan can I follow?

Enter Campley.

Camp. Follow my advice, Narcissa, by all means.
Enlist with me, under the best banners in the world.
General Hymen for my money ! little Cupid's his drum-
mer: he has been beating a round rub-a-dub on our
hearts, and we have only to obey the word of command,
fall into the ranks of matrimony, and march through life
together.
  " *Nar.* Halt! halt, Captain ! You march too quick;
besides, you make matrimony a mere parade."
  " *Camp.* Faith, I believe, many make it so at present.
But we are volunteers, Narcissa ! and I am for actual
service, I promise you."
  Nar. Then consider our situation.
  Camp. That has been duly consider'd. In short, the
case stands exactly thus—your intended spouse is all for
money: I am all for love: He is a rich rogue; I am
rather a poor honest fellow. He wou'd pocket your fortune; I will take you without a fortune in your pocket.
  " *Nar.* But where's Mr. Inkle's view of interest ?
Hasn't he run away from me ?
  " *Camp.* And I am ready to run away *with* you——
" you won't always meet with such an offer on an emer-
" gency."

                                                        Nar.

Nar. Oh! I am fenfible of the favour, moft gallant Captain Campley; and my father, no doubt, will be very much oblig'd to you.

Camp. Aye, there's the devil of it! Sir Chriftopher Curry's confounded good character---knocks me up at once. Yet I am not acquainted with him neither; not known to him, even by fight; being here only as a private gentleman on a vifit to my old relation, out of regimentals, and fo forth; and not introduc'd to the Governor as other-officers of the place: But then the report of his hofpitality---his odd, blunt, whimfical friendfhip---his whole behaviour-------

Nar. All ftare you in the face; eh, Campley?

Camp. They do till they put me out of countenance: But then again, when I ftare *you* in the face, I can't think I have any reafon to be afham'd of my proceedings.---I ftick here between my Love and my Principle, like a fong between a toaft and a fentiment.

Nar. And if your love and your principle were put in the fcales, you doubt which wou'd weigh moft?

Camp. Oh, no! I fhou'd act like a rogue, and let principle kick the beam: For love, Narciffa, is as heavy as lead, and like a bullet from a piftol, cou'd never go thro' the heart, if it wanted weight.

Nar. Or rather like the piftol itfelf, that often *goes off* without any harm done. Your fire muft end in fmoke, I believe.

Camp. Never, whilft------

Nar. Nay, a truce to proteftations at prefent. What fignifies talking to *me*, when you have fuch oppofition from others? Why hover about the city, inftead of boldly attacking the guard? Wheel about, captain! face the enemy! March! Charge! Rout 'em---Drive 'em before you, and then------

Camp. And then---

Nar. Lud ha' mercy on the poor city!

SONG.

SONG.——RONDEAU. &c.

Since 'tis vain to think of flying.

Mars wou'd oft, his conquest over,
    To the Cyprian Goddess yield;
Venus gloried in a lover,
Who, like him, cou'd brave the field.
                    Mars wou'd oft, &c.

II.

In the cause of battles hearty,
    Still the God wou'd strive to prove,
He who fac'd an adverse party,
    Fittest was to meet his love.
                    Mars wou'd oft, &c.

III.

Hear then, Captains, ye who bluster,
    Hear the God of War declare,
Cowards never can pass muster;
    Courage only wins the fair.
                    Mars wou'd oft, &c.

Enter Patty, *hastily.*

Patty. Oh lud, Ma'am, I'm frighten'd out of my
wits! sure as I'm alive, Ma'am, Mr. Inkle is not dead;
I saw his man, Ma'am, just now, coming ashore in a
boat with other passengers, from the vessel that's come to
the island.

" *Nar.* Then one way or other I must determine.
" *Patty.* But, pray Ma'am, don't tell the Captain;
" I'm sure he'll stick poor Trudge in his passion; and
" he's the best natur'd, peaceable, kind, loving soul in
" the world." 　　　　　　　　　　　　[*Exit* Patty.
Nar. (*to Camp.*) Look'ye, Mr. Campley, something
has happen'd which makes me wave ceremonies.---If you
                                                    mean

mean to apply to my father, remember that delays are dangerous.

Camp. Indeed!

Nar. I mayn't be always in the same mind, you know. (*Smiling.*)

Camp. Nay then----Gad, I'm almost afraid too--but living in this state of doubt is torment. I'll e'en put a good face on the matter; cock my hat; make my bow; and try to reason the Governor into compliance. Faint heart never won a fair Lady.

S O N G.

Why shou'd I vain fears discover,
Prove a dying, sighing swain?
Why turn shilly-shally lover,
Only to prolong my pain?

II.

When we woo the dear enslaver,
Boldly ask and she will grant;
How should we obtain a favour,
But by telling what we want?

III.

Should the nymph be found complying,
Nearly then the battle's won;
Parents think 'tis vain denying,
When half our work is fairly done.

[*Exeunt.*

Enter Trudge *and* Wowski (*as from the ship*) *with a dirty runner to one of the inns.*

Run. This way, Sir; if you will let me recommend——

Trudge. Come along, Wows! Take care of your furs, and your feathers, my girl.

E   *Wows.*

Wowf. Iſs.

Trudge. That's right.---Somebody might ſteal 'em, perhaps.

Wowf., Steal!---What that?

Trudge. Oh Lord! ſee what one loſes by not being born in a Chriſtian country.

Run. If you wou'd, Sir, but mention to your maſter, the houſe that belongs to my maſter; the beſt accommodations on the quay.---

Trudge. What's your ſign, my lad?

Run. The Crown, Sir.---Here it is.

Trudge. Well, get us a room for half an hour, and we'll come: and harkee! let it be light and airy, d'ye hear? My maſter has been us'd to your open apartments lately.

Run. Depend on it.---Much oblig'd to you, Sir.
            [*Exit.*

Wowf. Who be that fine man? He great Prince?

Trudge. A Prince---Ha! ha!---No, not quite a Prince---but he belongs to the Crown. But how do you like this, Wows? Iſn't it fine?

Wowf. Wonder!

Trudge. Fine men, eh!

Wowf. Iſs! all white; like you.

Trudge. Yes, all the fine men are like me: As different from your people as powder and ink, or paper and blacking.

Wowf. And fine lady---Face like ſnow.

Trudge. What! the fine ladies complexions? Oh, yes, exactly; for too much heat very often diſſolves 'em! Then their dreſs, too.

Wowf. Your countrymen dreſs ſo?

Trudge. Better, better a great deal. Why, a young flaſhy Engliſhman will ſometimes carry a whole fortune on his back. But did you mind the women? All here--- and there; (*pointing before and behind*) they have it all from us in England.---And then the fine things they carry on their heads, Wowſki.

Wowf. Iſs. One Lady carry good fiſh---ſo fine, ſhe call every body to look at her.

                                Trudge.

Trudge. Pſhaw! an old woman, bawling flounders. But the fine girls we meet here on the quay---ſo round, and ſo plump!

Wowſ. You not love me now.

Trudge. Not love you! Zounds have not I given you proofs?

Wowſ. Iſs. Great many: But now you get here, you forget your poor Wowſki!

Trudge. Not I: I'll ſtick to you like wax.

Wowſ. Ah! I fear! What make you love me now?

Trudge. Gratitude, to be ſure.

Wowſ. What that?

Trudge. Ha! this it is now to live without educa-tion. The poor dull devils of her country are all in the practice of gratitude, without finding out what it means; while we can tell the meaning of it, with little or no prac-tice at all.---Lord, Lord, what a fine advantage Chriſ-tain-learning is! Hark'ee, Wows!

Wowſ. Iſs.

Trudge. Now we've accompliſh'd our landing, I'll accompliſh you. You remember the inſtructions I gave you on the voyage?

Wowſ. Iſs.

Trudge. Let's ſee, now---What are you to do, when I introduce you to the Nobility, Gentry, and others--- of my acquaintance?

Wowſ. Make believe ſit down; then get up.

Trudge. Let me ſee you do it. [*She makes a low curteſey.* Very well! And how are you to recommend yourſelf, when you have nothing to ſay, amongſt all our great friends?

Wowſ. Grin---ſhew my teeth.

Trudge. Right! they'll think you've liv'd with people of faſhion. But ſuppoſe you meet an old ſhabby friend in misfortune, that you don't wiſh to be ſeen to ſpeak to ---what wou'd you do?

Wowſ. Look blind---not ſee him.

Trudge. Why wou'd you do that?

Wowſ. 'Cauſe I can't bear ſee good friend in diſtreſs.

Trudge. That's a good girl! and I wiſh every body cou'd boaſt of ſo kind a motive for ſuch curſed cruel behaviour.--Lord! how some of your flashy bankers clerks have *cut* me in Threadneedle-street.--But come, tho' we have got among fine folks here, in an English settlement, I won't be asham'd of my old acquaintance: yet, for my own part, I should not be sorry, now, to see my old friend with a new face.----Odsbobs! I see Mr. Inkle---Go in, Wows ;---call for what you like best.

Wows. Then, I call for you; ah! I fear I not see you often now. But you come soon---

S O N G.

Remember when we walk'd alone,
    And heard so gruff the lion growl;
And when the moon so bright it shone,
    We saw the wolf look up and howl;
I led you well, safe to our cell,
      While tremblingly
       You said to me,
---And kiss'd so sweet—dear Wowski *tell,*
      How cou'd I live without ye?

II.

But now you come across the sea,
    And tell me here no monsters roar;
You'll walk alone and leave poor me,
    When wolves to fright you howl no more.
But, ah! think well on our old cell,
      Where tremblingly
       You kiss'd poor me—
Perhaps you'll say---dear Wowski *tell,*
      How can I live without ye?
          [Exit *Wowski.*

Trudge. Eh! oh! my master's talking to somebody on the quay: who have we here!

Enter

Enter Firſt Planter.

Plant. Hark'ee, young man! Is that young Indian of your's going to our market?

Trudge. Not ſhe---ſhe never went to market in all her life.

Plant. I mean is ſhe for our ſale of ſlaves? Our Black Fair?

Trudge. A Black Fair! Ha! ha! ha! You hold it on a brown green, I ſuppoſe.

Plant. She's your ſlave, I take it?

Trudge. Yes; and I'm her humble ſervant, I take it.

Plant. Aye, aye, natural enough at ſea.---But at how much do you value her?

Trudge. Juſt as much as ſhe has ſav'd me---My own life.

Plant. Pſhaw! you mean to ſell her?

Trudge. (*Staring*) Zoûnds! what a devil of a fellow! Sell Wows!---my poor, dear, dingy wife!

Plant. Come, come, I've heard your ſtory from the ſhip.---Don't let's haggle; I'll bid as fair as any trader amongſt us: But no tricks upon travellers, young man, to raiſe your price.---Your wife, indeed! Why, ſhe's no Chriſtian?

Trudge. No; but I am; ſo I ſhall do as I'd be done by, Maſter *Black-Market:* and, if you were a good one yourſelf, you'd know, that fellow feeling for a poor body, who wants your help, is the nobleſt mark of our religion. ---I wou'dn't be articled clerk to ſuch a fellow for the world.

Plant. Hey-day! The booby's in love with her! Why, ſure friend, you wou'd not live here with a Black?

Trudge. Plague on't; there it is. I ſhall be laugh'd out of my honeſty, here.---But you may be jogging, friend! I may feel a little queer, perhaps, at ſhewing her face---but, dam'me, if ever I do any thing to make me aſham'd of ſhewing my own.

Plant. Why, I tell you, her very complexion.---

Trudge. Rot her complexion.---I'll tell you what, Mr. Faïr Trader: If your head and heart were to change places,
places,

places, I've a notion you'd be as black in the face as an ink-bottle.

Plant. Pſhaw! The fellow's a fool---a rude raſcal--- he ought to be ſent back to the ſavages again. He's not fit to live among us Chriſtians.   [*Exit* Planter.

" *Trudge.* Chriſtians! ah! tender ſouls they are to be ſure."

S O N G.

American Tune.

" *Chriſtians are ſo good, they ſay,*
    Tender ſouls as e'er can be!
Let them credit it who may;
    What they're made of let us ſee.

II.

" *Chriſtian drovers, charming trade!*
    Who ſo careful cattle drive;
And the tender Chriſtian maid,
    Sweetly ſkinning eels alive.

III.

" *Tender toniſh dames who take*
    Whip in hand, and drive like males,
Have their ponies nick'd---to make
    The pretty creatures cock their tails.

IV.

" *Chriſtian boys will ſhy at cocks,*
    Worry dogs, hunt cats, kill flies;
Chriſtian Lords will learn to box,
    And give their noble friends black eyes."

Oh, here he is at laſt.

Enter

Enter Inkle, *and another* Planter.

Inkle. Nay, Sir, I underſtand your cuſtoms well: your Indian markets are not unknown to me.

2d Plant. And, as you ſeem to underſtand buſineſs, I need not tell you that diſpatch is the ſoul of it. Her name you ſay is---

Inkle. Yarico: But urge this no more, I beg you. I muſt not liſten to it. For to ſpeak freely, her anxious care of me demands, that here,---though here it may ſeem ſtrange,---I ſhould avow my love for her.

Plant. Lord help you, for a merchant!--" What a " pretty figure you would cut upon Change"--It's the firſt time I ever heard a trader talk of love; except indeed the love of trade, and the love of the *Sweet Molly,* my ſhip.

Inkle. Then, Sir, you cannot feel my ſituation.

Plant. Oh yes, I can! We have a hundred ſuch caſes juſt after a voyage; but they never laſt long on land. It's amazing how conſtant a young man is in a ſhip! But, in two words, Will you diſpoſe of her, or no?

Inkle. In two words then, meet me here at noon, and we'll ſpeak further on this ſubject: and left you think I trifle with your buſineſs, hear why I wiſh this pauſe. Chance threw me, on my paſſage to your iſland, among a ſavage people. Deſerted,---defenceleſs,---cut off from my companions,---my life at ſtake---to this young creature I owe my preſervation;---ſhe found me, like a dying bough, torn from its kindred branches; which, as it droop'd, ſhe moiſten'd with her tears.

Plant. Nay, nay, talk like a man of this world.

Inkle. Your patience.---And yet your interruption goes to my preſent feelings; for on our ſail to this your iſland---the thoughts of time miſpent---doubt---fears--- or call it what you will---have much perplex'd me; and as your ſpires aroſe, reflections ſtill roſe with them; for here, Sir, lie my intereſts, great connections, and other weighty matters---which now I need not mention---

Plant. But which her preſence here will mar.

Inkle.

Inkle. Even fo---And yet the gratitude I owe her!

Plant. Pfhaw! So becaufe fhe preferv'd your life, your gratitude is, to make you give up all you have to live upon.

Inkle. Why in that light indeed---This never ftruck me yet. I'll think on't.

Plant. Aye, aye, do fo---Why what return can the wench wifh more than taking her from a wild, idle, fa-vage people, and providing for her, here, with reputable hard work, in a genteel, polifhed, tender, chriftian country?

Inkle. Well, Sir, at noon——

Plant. I'll meet you---but remember, young gentle-man, you muft get her off your hands---you muft in-deed.---I fhall have her a bargain, I fee that---your fervant!---Zounds how late it is---but never be put out of your way for a woman---I muft run---my wife will play the devil with me for keeping breakfaft.   [*Exit.*

Inkle. Trudge.

Trudge. Sir!

Inkle. Have you provided a proper apartment?

Trudge. Yes, Sir, at the Crown here; a neat, fpruce room they tell me. You have not feen fuch a convenient lodging this good while I believe.

Inkle. Are there no better inns in the town?

Trudge. Um!----Why there's the Lion, I hear, and the Bear, and the Boar---but we faw them at the door of all our late lodgings, and found but bad accom-modations within, Sir.

Inkle. Well, run to the end of the quay, and con-duct Yarico hither. The road is ftraight before you: You can't mifs it.

Trudge. Very well, Sir. What a fine thing it is to turn one's back on a mafter, without running into a wolf's belly! One can follow one's nofe on a meffage here, and be fure it won't be bit off by the way. [*Exit.*

Inkle. Let me reflect a little. "This honeft planter coun-"cils well." Part with her---" What is there in it which "cannot eafily be juftified?" Juftified !---" Pfhaw"---My intereft, honour, engagements to Narciffa, all de-mand it. My father's precepts too---I can remember,

3   when

when I was a boy, what pains he took to mould me!---School'd me from morn to night---and ftill the burthen of his fong was---Prudence! Prudence, Thomas, and you'll rife.---Early he taught me numbers; which he faid---and he faid rightly---wou'd give me a quick view of lofs and profit; and banifh from my mind thofe idle impulfes of paffion, which mark young thoughtlefs fpendthrifts. His maxims rooted in my heart, and as I grew---*they* grew; till I was reckon'd, among our friends, a fteady, fober, folid, good young man; and all the neighbours call'd me *the prudent Mr. Thomas.* And fhall I now, at once, kick down the character, which I have rais'd fo warily?---Part with her,---"fell her,"---The thought once ftruck me in our cabin, as fhe lay fleeping by me; but, in her flumbers, fhe paft her arm around me, murmur'd a bleffing on my name, and broke my meditations.

Enter Yarico *and* Trudge.

Yar. My Love!

Trudge. I have been fhewing her all the wigs and bales of goods we met on the quay, Sir.

Yar. Oh! I have feafted my eyes on wonders.

Trudge. And I'll go feaft on a flice of beef, in the inn here.   [*Exit.*

Yar. My mind has been fo bufy, that I almoft forgot even you. I wifh you had ftaid with me--You wou'd have feen fuch fights!

Inkle. Thofe fights are grown familiar to *me*, Yarico.

Yar. And yet I wifh they were not---You might partake my pleafures---but now again, methinks, I will not wifh fo---for with too much gazing; you might neglect poor *Yarico.*

Inkle. Nay, nay, my care is ftill for you.

Yar. I'm fure it is: and if I thought it was not, I'd tell you tales about our poor, old, grot---Bid you remember our Palm-tree near the brook, where in the fhade you often ftretched yourfelf, while I would take your head

E   upon

upon my lap, and sing my love to sleep.   I know you'll love me then.

SONG.

Our grotto was the sweetest place!
  The bending bows, with fragrance blowing,
Would check the brook's impetuous pace,
  Which murmur'd to be stopt from flowing.
'Twas there we met, and gazed our fill.
Ah! think on this, and love me still.

II.

'Twas then my bosom first knew fear,
  —Fear, to an Indian maid a stranger—
The war song, arrows, hatchet, spear,
  All warn'd me of my lover's danger.
For him did cares my bosom fill;
Ah! think on this, and love me still.

III.

"For him, by day, with care conceal'd,
  "To search for food I climb'd the mountain;
"And when the night no form reveal'd,
  "Jocund we sought the bubbling fountain.
"Then, then would joy my bosom fill;
"Ah! think on this, and love me still."   [Exeunt.

SCENE, An apartment in the house of Sir Christopher
Curry.

Enter Sir Christopher and Medium.

Sir Chr.   I tell you, old Medium, you are all wrong.
Plague on your doubts! Inkle shall have my Narcissa.
                                                                 Poor

Poor fellow ! I dare fay he's finely chagrined at this tem-
porary parting---Eat up with the blue devils, I warrant.

Med. Eat up by the black devils, I warrant; for I
left him in hellifh hungry company.

Sir. Chr. Pfhaw ! he'll arrive with the next veffel,
depend on't---befides, have I not hád this in view ever
fince they were children ? I muft and will have it fo, I
tell you. Is not it, as it were, a marriage made above ?
They *fhall* meet, I'm pofitive.

Med. Shall they ? Then they muft meet where the
marriage was made ; for hang me, if I think it will ever
happen below.

Sir Chr. Ha !---and if that is the cafe---hang me,
if I think you'll ever be at the celebration of it.

Med. Yet, let me tell you, Sir Chriftopher Curry,
my chara&ter is as unfullied as a fheet of white paper.

Sir Chr. Well faid, old fool's-cap ! and it's as mere
a blank as a fheet of white paper. " It bears the traces
" of neither a bad or a good hand upon it ! Zounds ! I
" had rather be à walking libel on honefty, than fit down
" a blank in the library of the world. ·

" *Med.* Well, it is not for me to boaft of virtues :
" That's a vice I never give into.

" *Sir Chr.* Your virtues ! zounds, what are they ?

" *Med.* I am not addi&ted to paffion---that at leaft,
" Sir Chriftopher---"

Sir Chr. Is like all your other virtues--A negative
one. You are honeft, old Medium, by comparifon, juft
as a fellow fenténç'd to tranfportation is happier than his
companion condemned to the gallows---Very worthy,
becaufe you are no rogue ; " a good friend, becaufe you
ne ver bear malice ;" Tender hearted, becaufe you never
go to fires and executions ; and an affe&tionate father and
hufband, becaufe you never pinch your children, or
kick your wife out of bed.

Med. And that, as the world goes, is more than every
man can fay for himfelf. Yet, fince you force me to
fpeak, my pofitive qualities---but, no matter---you remember me in London ; " and know, there was fcarcely

" a laudable inftitution in town, without my name in the
" lift.   Hav'n't I given more tickets to recommend the
" lopping off legs than any Governor of our Hofpital?
" and" didn't I as Member of the Humane Society,
bring a man out of the New River, who, it was afterwards found, had done me an injury?

Sir Chr. And, dam'me, If I wou'd not kick any man
into the New River that had done me an injury. There's
the difference of our honefty.   Oons! if you want to be
an honeft fellow, act from the impulfe of nature.   Why,
you have no more gall than a pigeon.

" *Med.*   That, I think, is pretty evident in my pri-
" vate life.---Patience, patience you muft own, Sir
" Chriftopher, is a virtue.   And I have fat and feen my
" beft friends abus'd, with as much quiet patience as any
" Chriftian in Chriftendom.

" *Sir Chr.*   And I'd quarrel with any man, that
" abus'd my friend in my company.   Offending my ears
" is as bad as boxing them."

Med. " Ha!" You're always fo hafty; amongft the
hodge-podge of your foibles, paffion is always predomi-
nant.

Sir Chr.   So much the better.---" A natural man,
" unfeafoned with paffion, is as uncommon as a difh of
" hodge-podge without pepper; and devilifh infipid too,
" old Medium."---Foibles, quotha? foibles are foils that
" give additional luftre to the gems of virtue.   You
have not fo many foils as I, perhaps.

Med.   And, what's more, I don't want 'em, Sir
Chriftopher, I thank you.

Sir Chr.   Very true; for the devil a gem have you
to fet off with 'em.

Med.   Well, well; I never mention errors; that, I
flatter myfelf, is no difagreeable quality.---It don't become me to fay you are hot.

Sir Chr. 'Sblood! but it does become you: it becomes every man, efpecially an Englifhman, to fpeak
the dictatss of his heart.

SONG.

S O N G.

     "*O give me your plain dealing Fellows,*
      "*Who never from honesty shrink;*
     "*Not thinking on all they should tell us,*
     "*But telling us all that they think.*

II.

     "*Truth from man flows like wine from a bottle,*
      "*His free spoken heart's a full cup;*
     "*But, when truth sticks half way in the throttle,*
     "*Man's worse than a bottle cork'd up.*

III.

     "*Complaisance, is a Gingerbread creature——*
      "*Us'd for shew, like a watch, by each spark;*
     "*But truth is a golden repeater.*
     "*That sets a man right in the dark.*"

   "*Med.* But suppose his heart dictates to any one to
"knock up your friend, Sir Christopher?
   "*Sir Chr.* Eh!---why---then it becomes me to
"knock him down.
   "*Med.* Mercy on us! If that was the consequence
"of scandal in England now-a-days, all our fine gentle-
"men wou'd cut each others throats over a bottle; and,
"if extended to the card tables, our routs wou'd be
"fuller of black eyes, than black aces."

Enter Servant.

Serv. An English vessel, Sir, is just arriv'd in the
harbour.
   Sir Chr. A vessel! Odd's my life!---Now for the
news---If it is but as I hope---Any dispatches?
   Serv. This letter, Sir, brought by a sailor from the
quay.   [*Exit.*
                                     "*Sir*

" *Sir Chr.* Now for it ! If Inkle is but amongst
" em---Zounds ! I'm all in a flutter ; my hand shakes
" like an aspin leaf ; and you, you old fool, are as stiff
" and steady as an oak.   Why ar'n't you all tiptoe---
" all nerves ?——

" *Med.*   Well, read, Sir Christopher."

Sir Chr. (*opening the letter.*) Huzza ! here it is.
He's safe---safe and found at Barbadoes.

(Reading.)——*Sir,*

My father, Mr. Inkle is just arriv'd in your harbour.
Here, read, read ! old Medium——

Med. (*Reading.*) Um'---*Your harbour ;---we were
taken up by an English vessel on the 14th ult*[o]*. He only waits
till I have puff'd his hair, to pay his respects to you, and
Miss Narcissa : In the mean time, he has order'd me to
brush up this letter for your honour from*

Your humble Servant, to command,

Timothy Trudge.

Sir Chr.   Hey day ! Here's a stile ! the voyage has
jumbled the fellow's brains out of their places ; the water has made his head turn round.   But no matter ; mine
turns round, too.   I'll go and prepare Narcissa directly ;
they shall be married, slap-dash, as soon as he comes
from the quay.   From Neptune to Hymen ; from the
hammock to the bridal bed—Ha ! old boy !

Med.   Well, well ; don't flurry yourself—you're so
hot !

Sir Chr.   Hot ! blood, an't I in the West Indies !
An't I Governor of Barbadoes ? He shall have her as
soon as he sets his foot on shore.   " But plague on't, he's
so slow.—"She shall rise to him Like Venus out of the
sea.   His hair puff'd ! He ought to have been puffing,
here, out of breath, by this time.

Med. Very true ; but Venus's husband is always sup-
posed to be lame, you know, Sir Christopher.

Sir

Sir Chr. Well, now do, my good fellow, run down to the fhore, and fee what detains him. [*Hurrying him off.*
Med. Well, well; I will, I will. [*Exit.*
Sir Chr. In the mean time, I'll get ready Narciffa, and all fhall be concluded in a fecond. My heart's fet upon it.----Poor fellow! after all his rumbles, and tumbles, and jumbles, and fits of defpair---I fhall be re-joic'd to fee him. I have not feen him fince he was that high.—But, zounds! he's fo tardy!

Enter Servant.

Serv. A ftrange Gentleman, Sir, come from the quay, defires to fee you.
Sir Chr. From the quay? Od's my life!---'Tis he---'Tis Inkle! Shew him up, directly. (*Exit Servant.*) The rogue *is* expeditious after all.----I'm fo happy.

Enter Campley.

My dear Fellow! [*Embracing him---fhakes hands.*] I'm rejoic'd to fee you. Welcome! welcome here, with all my foul!
Camp. This reception, Sir Chriftopher, is beyond my warmeft wifhes---Unknown to you——
Sir Chr. Aye, aye; we fhall be better acquainted by and by. Well, and how, eh! Tell me!---But old Medium and I have talk'd over your affair a hundred times a day, ever fince Narciffa arriv'd.
Camp. You furprize me! Are you then really acquainted with the whole affair?
Sir Chr. Every tittle.
Camp. And, can you, Sir, pardon what is paft?---
Sir Chr. Pooh! how could you help it?
Camp. Very true---failing in the fame fhip---and---
Sir Chr. Aye, aye;-but we have had a hundred con-" jectures about you. Your defpair and diftrefs, and all " that---Your's muft have been a damn'd fituation, to " fay the truth.
Camp. " Crüel indeed, Sir Chriftopher! and I " flatter myfelf will move your compaffion. I have
" been

" been almoſt inclin'd to deſpair, indeed, as you ſay,"
---when you conſider the paſt ſtate of my mind---
the black proſpect before me.——

  Sir Chr. Ha! ha! Black enough, I dare ſay.

  Camp. The difficulty I have felt in bringing myſelf
face to face to you.

  Sir Chr. That I am convinc'd of---but I knew you
wou'd come the firſt opportunity.

  Camp. Very true: yet the diſtance between the Governor of Barbadoes and myſelf. [*Bowing.*]

  Sir Chr. Yes——a deviliſh way aſunder.

  Camp. Granted, Sir: which has diſtreſs'd me with
the cruelleſt doubts as to our meeting.

  Sir Chr. It was a toſs up.

  Camp. The old Gentleman ſeems deviliſh kind.---
Now to ſoften him. [*Aſide*] Perhaps, Sir, in your
younger days, you may have been in the ſame ſituation yourſelf.

  Sir Chr. Who? I! 'ſblood! no, never in my life.

  Camp. I wiſh you had, with all my ſoul, Sir Chriſtopher.

  Sir Chr. Upon my ſoul, Sir, I am very much ob-
liged to you. (*Bowing*)

  Camp. As what I now mention might have greater
weight with you.

  Sir Chr. Pooh! prithee! I tell you I pitied you
from the bottom of my heart.

  Camp. Indeed! " Had you but been kind enough
" to have ſent to me, how happy ſhould I have been
" in attending your commands!

  " *Sir Chr.* I believe you wou'd, egad---ha! ha!
" ſent to you! Very well! ha! ha! ha! A dry
" rogue! You'd have been ready enough to come my
" boy, I dare ſay. (*Laughing.*)

  Camp. " But now, Sir;" if, with your leave, I may
ſtill venture to mention Miſs Narciſſa----

  Sir Chr. An impatient, ſenſible young dog! like
me to a hair! Set your heart at reſt, my boy. She's
your's; your's before to-morrow morning.

  Camp. Amazement! I can ſcarce believe my ſenſes.

                      Sir

Sir Chr. Zounds! you ought to be out of your fenfes; but difpatch---make fhort work of it, ever while you live, my boy.

Enter Narciffa *and* Patty.

Here, girl: here's your fwain. [*To* Nar.

Camp. I juft parted with my Narciffa, on the quay, Sir.

Sir Chr. Did you! Ah, fly dog---had a meeting before you came to the old Gentleman.---But here--- Take him, and make much of him--and, for fear of fur- ther feparations, you fhall e'en be tack'd together di- rectly. What fay you, girl?

Camp. Will my Narciffa confent to my happinefs?

Nar. I always obey my father's commands, with pleafure, Sir.

Sir Chr. Od! I'm fo happy, I hardly know which way to turn; but we'll have the carriage directly; drive down to the quay; trundle old Spintext into church; and hey for matrimony!

Camp. With all my heart, Sir Chriftopher; the fooner the better.

Sir CHRISTOPHER, CAMPLEY, NARCISSA, PATTY.

Sir Chr. *Your Colinettes, and Arriettes,*
 Your Damons of the grove,
Who like Fallals, and Paftorals,
 Wafte years in love!
But modern folks know better jokes,
 And, courting once begun,
To church they hop at once---and pop---
 Egad, all's done!

All. *In life we prance a country dance,*
 Where every couple ftands;
Their partners fet---a while curvett---
 But foon join hands.

    G   Nar.

Nar.
> When at our feet, so trim and neat,
>   The powder'd lover sues,
> He vows he dies, the lady sighs,
>   But can't refuse.
> Ah! how can she, unmov'd, e'er see
>   Her swain his death incur?
> If once the Squire is seen expire,
>   He lives with her.

All.   In life, &c. &c.

Patty.   When John and Bet are fairly met,
>   John boldly tries his luck;
> He steals a buss, without more fuss,
>   The bargain's struck.
> Whilst things below are going so,
>   Is Betty pray to blame?
> Who knows, up stairs, her mistress fares
>   Just, just the same.

All.   In life we prance, &c. &c.   [Exeunt.

End of the SECOND ACT.

ACT III.

SCENE I. *The Quay.*

Enter Patty.

MERCY on us! what a walk I have had of it! Well, matters go on swimmingly at the governor's--The old gentleman has order'd the carriage, and the young couple will be whisk'd, here, to the church, in a quarter of an hour. My business is to prevent young fobersides, Young Inkle, from appearing, to interrupt the ceremony. ---Ha! here's the Crown, where I hear he is hous'd. So now to find Trudge, and trump up a story, in the true stile of a chambermaid. *(Goes into the house.) (Patty within)* I tell you it don't signify, and I will come up. *(Trudge within.)* But it does signify, and you can't come up.

Re-enter Patty, *with* Trudge.

Patty. You had better say at once, I shan't.

Trudge. Well then you shan't.

Patty. Savage! Pretty behaviour you have pick'd up amongst the Hottypots! Your London civility, like London itself, will soon be lost in smoke, Mr. Trudge; and the politeness you have studied so long in Threadneedle-street, blotted out by the blacks you have been living with.

Trudge. No such thing; I practis'd my politeness all the while I was in the woods. Our very lodging taught me good manners; for I could never bring myself to go into it without bowing.

G 2

Patty.

Patty. Don't tell me. A mighty civil reception you give a body, truly, after a six weeks parting!

Trudge. Gad, you're right; I am a little out here, to be sure. (*Kisses her.*) Well, how do you do?

Patty. Pshaw! Fellow! I want none of your kisses.

Trudge. Oh! very well---I'll take it again. (*Offers to kiss her.*)

Patty. Be quiet. I want to see Mr. Inkle. I have a message to him from Miss Narcissa. I shall get a sight of him, now, I believe.

Trudge. May be not. He's a little busy at present.

Patty. Busy---ha! Plodding! What he's at his multiplication again?

Trudge. Very likely; so it would be a pity to interrupt him, you know.

Patty. Certainly; and the whole of my business was to prevent his hurrying himself---Tell him, we shan't be ready to receive him at the Governor's till to-morrow, d'ye hear?

Trudge. No?

Patty. No! Things are not prepared. The place isn't in order; and the servants have not had proper notice of the arrival.

Trudge. Oh! let me alone to give the servants notice--Rat--Tat--Tat--It's all the notice we had in Threadneedle-street of the arrival of a visitor.

Patty. Threadneedle-street! Threadneedle nonsense! I'd have you to know we do every thing, here, with an air. Matters have taken another turn---Stile! Stile, Sir, is required here, I promise you.

Trudge. Turn--Stile! And pray what stile will serve your turn now, Madam Patty?

Patty. A due dignity and decorum, to be sure. Sir Christopher intends Mr. Inkle, you know, for his son-in-law, and must receive him in public form, (which can't be till to-morrow morning) for the honor of his governorship: why the whole island will ring of it.

Trudge. The devil it will!

Patty. Yes; they've talk'd of nothing but my mistress's beauty and fortune, for these six weeks. Then he'll be introduced to the bride, you know.

Trudge.

Trudge. O, my poor master!

Patty. Then a publick breakfast; then a proceffion; then---if nothing happens to prevent it, he'll get into church and be married in a crack.

Trudge. Then he'll get into a damn'd fcrape, in a crack.

Patty. Hey-day! a fcrape! The holy ftate of matrimony!

Trudge. Yes; it's plaguy holy; and many of its votaries, as in other holy ftates, live in repentance and mortification. Ah! poor Madam Yarico! My poor pilgarlick of a mafter, what will become of him? (*Half afide.*)

Patty. Why, what's the matter with the booby?

Trudge. Nothing, nothing---he'll be hang'd for poli-bigamy.

Patty. Polly who?

Trudge. It muft out---Patty!

Patty. Well?

Trudge. Can you keep a fecret?

Patty. Try me!

Trudge. Then [*Whifpering*] My mafter keeps a girl.

Patty. Oh monftrous! another woman?

Trudge. As fure as one and one make two.

Patty. [*Afide.*] Rare news for my miftrefs!---Why I can hardly believe it: the grave, fly, fteady, fober Mr. Inkle, do fuch a thing!

Trudge. Pooh! it's always your fly, fober fellows, that go the moft after the girls.

Patty. Well; I fhould fooner fufpect you.

Trudge. Me? Oh Lord! he! he!---Do you think any fmart, tight, little black eyed wench, wou'd be ftruck with my figure? [*Conceitedly.*]

Patty. Pfhaw! never mind your figure. Tell me how it happen'd?

Trudge. You fhall hear: when the fhip left us afhore, my mafter turn'd as pale as a fheet of paper. It ifh't every body that's bleft with courage, Patty.

Patty. True!

Trudge. However, I bid him cheer up; told him, to ftick to my elbow: took the lead, and began our march.

Patty. Well?

Trudge. We hadn't gone far, when a damn'd one-eyed black boar, that grinn'd like a devil, came down the hill in jog trot! My mafter melted as faft as a pot of pomatum!

Patty. Mercy on us!

Trudge. But what does I do, but whips out my defk knife, that I us'd to cut the quills with at home; met the monfter, and flit up his throat like a pen---The boar bled like a pig.

Patty. Lord! Trudge, what a great traveller you are!

Trudge. Yes; I remember we fed on the flitch for a week.

Patty. Well, well; but the Lady.

Trudge. The Lady? O, true. By and by we came to a cave---a large hollow room, under ground, like a warehoufe in the Adelphi—Well; there we were half an hour, before I could get him to go in; there's no accounting for fear you know. At laft, in we went, to a place hung round with fkins, as it might be a Furrier's fhop; and there was a fine Lady, fnoring on a bow and arrows.

Patty. What, all alone?

Trudge. Eh!---No---no---no. Hum---She had a young lion by way of a lap-dog.

Patty. Gemini! what did you do?

Trudge. Gave her a jog, and fhe open'd her eyes--- fhe ftruck my mafter immediately.

Patty. Mercy on us! with what?

Trudge. With her beauty, you Ninny, to be fure: and they foon brought matters to bear. The wolves witnefs'd the contract---I gave her away---The crows croak'd Amen; and we had board and lodging for nothing.

Patty. And this is fhe he has brought to Barbadoes?

Trudge. The fame.

Patty. Well; and tell me Trudge;---fhe's pretty, you fay--Is fhe fair or brown? or——

Trudge. Um! fhe's a good comely copper.

Patty. How! a Tawney?

Trudge.

Trudge. Yes; quite dark; but very elegant; like a Wedge-wood tea-pot.

Patty. Oh! the monster! the filthy fellow! Live with a black-a-moor!

Trudge. Why there's no great harm in't, I hope.

Patty. Faugh! I wou'dn't let him kiss me for the world: he'd make my face all smutty.

Trudge. Zounds! you are mighty nice all of a sudden; but I'd have you to know, Madam Patty, that Blackamoor Ladies, as you call 'em, are some of the very few, whose complexions never rub off! S'bud, if they did, Wows and I shou'd have changed faces by this time---But mum; not a word for your life.

Patty. Not I! except to the Governor and family. [*Aside.*] But I must run--and, remember, Trudge, if your master has made a mistake here, he has himself to thank for his pains.

SONG.

Tho' lovers, like markfmen, all aim at the heart,
  Some hit wide of the mark, as we wenches all know;
But of all the bad shots, he's the worst in the art
  Who shoots at a pigeon, and kills a crow——O ho!
      Your master has kill'd a crow.

II.

When younkers go out, the first time in their lives,
  At random they shoot, and let fly as they go;
So your master, unskill'd how to level at wives,
  Has shot at a pigeon, and kill'd a crow.
      O ho! &c.

III.

Love and money thus wasted, in terrible trim!
  His powder is spent, and his shot running low:
Yet the pigeon he miss'd, I've a notion, with him
  Will never, for such a mistake, pluck a crow.
      No! no!
      Your master may keep his crow.

3   [*Exit Patty.*
                                       Trudge.

Trudge. Pfhaw! thefe girls are fo plaguy proud of their white and red! but I won't be fhamed out of Wows, that's flat. Mafter, to be fure, while we were in the foreft, taught Yarico to read, with his pencil and pocket-book. What then? Wows comes on fine and faft in her leffons. A little awkward at firft, to be fure. ---Ha! ha!---She's fo us'd to feed with her hands, that I can't get her to eat her victuals, in a genteel, Chriftian way, for the foul of me; when fhe has ftuck a morfel on her fork, fhe don't know how to guide it; but pops up her knuckles to her mouth, and the meat goes up to her ear. But, no matter---After all the fine, flafhy, London girls, Wowfki's the wench for my money.

S O N G.

A Clerk I was in London gay,
　　Jemmy linkum feedle,
And went in boots to fee the play,
　　Merry fiddlem tweedle.
I march'd the lobby, twirl'd my ftick,
　　Diddle, daddle, deedle;
The girls all cry'd, " He's quite the kick!"
　　Oh, Jemmy linkum feedle.

II.

Hey! for America I fail,
　　Yankee doodle deedle;
The failor boys cry'd, " fmoke his tail!"
　　Jemmy linkum feedle.
On Englifh belles I turn'd my back,
　　Diddle, daddle, deedle;
And got a foreign Fair, quite Black,
　　O twaddle, twaddle, tweedle!

III, *Your*

III.

Your London girls, with roguish trip,
       Wheedle, wheedle, wheedle,
May boaft their pouting under-lip,
       Fiddle, faddle, feedle.
My Wows wou'd beat a hundred fuch,
       Diddle, daddle, deedle,
Whofe upper-lip pouts twice as much,
       O, pretty double wheedle!

IV.

Rings I'll buy to deck her toes;
       Jemmy linkum feedle;
A feather fine fhall grace her nofe:
       Waving fidle feedle.
With jealoufy I ne'er fhall burft;
       Who'd fteal my bone of bone-a?
A white Othello, I can truft
       A dingy Defdemona.   [Exit.

SCENE II.   *A Room in the* Crown.

Enter Inkle.

I know not what to think---I have given her diftant
hints of parting; but ftill, fo ftrong her confidence in my
affection, fhe prattles on without regarding me. Poor
Yarico! I muft not---cannot quit her. When I wou'd
fpeak, her look, her mere fimplicity difarms me: I dare
not wound fuch innocence. Simplicity is like a fmiling
babe; which, to the ruffian, that wou'd murder it,
ftretching its little, naked, helplefs arms, pleads, fpeech-
lefs, its own caufe. And yet Narciffa's family——

H   *Enter*

Enter Trudge.

Trudge. There he is, like a beau befpeaking a coat---doubting which colour to chufe---Sir--

Inkle. What now?

Trudge. Nothing unexpected, Sir:---I hope you won't be angry.

Inkle. Angry!

Trudge. I'm forry for it; but I am come to give you joy, Sir!

Inkle. Joy!——of what!

Trudge. A wife, Sir; a white one.----I know it will vex you, but Mifs Narciffa means to make you happy to-morrow morning.

Inkle. To-morrow!

Trudge. Yes, fir; and as I have been out of employ, in both my capacities. lately, after I have drefs'd your hair, I may draw up the marriage articles.

Inkle. Whence comes your intelligence, fir?

Trudge. Patty told me all that has pafs'd in the Governor's family, on the quay, fir. Women, you know, can never keep a fecret. You'll be introduc'd in form, with the whole ifland to witnefs it.

Inkle. So public too!——Unlucky!

Trudge. There will be nothing but rejoicings in compliment to the wedding, fhe tells me; all noife and uproar! Married people like it, they fay.

Inkle. Strange! That I fhould be fo blind to my interest, as to be the only perfon this diftreffes!

Trudge. They are talking of nothing elfe but the match, it feems.

Inkle. Confufion! How can I, in honor, retract?

Trudge. And the bride's merits——

Inkle. True!---A fund of merits!---I wou'd not---but from neceffity---a cafe fo nice as this----I---wou'd not wifh to retract.

Trudge. Then they call her fo handfome.

Inkle. Very true! fo handfome! the whole world wou'd laugh at me: they'd call it folly to retract.

Trudge.

Trudge. And then they say so much of her fortune.

Inkle. O death! it would be *madness* to retract. Surely, my faculties have slept, and this long parting from my Narcissa, has blunted my sense of her accomplishments. 'Tis this alone makes me so weak, and wavering. I'll see her immediately. [*Going.*]

Trudge. Stay, stay, Sir; I am desir'd to tell you, the Governor won't open his gates to us till to-morrow morning, and is now making preparations to receive you at breakfast, with all the honours of matrimony.

Inkle. Well, be it so; it will give me time, at all events, to put my affairs in train.

Trudge. Yes; it's a short respite before execution; and if your honour was to go and comfort poor Madam Yarico——

Inkle. Damnation! Scoundrel, how dare you offer your advice?---I dread to think of her.

Trudge. I've done, Sir, I've done---But I know I should blubber over Wows all night, if I thought of parting with her in the morning.

Inkle. Insolence! begone, Sir!

Trudge. Lord, Sir, I only——

Inkle. Get down stairs, Sir, directly.

Trudge. [*Going out.*] Ah! you may well put your hand to your head; and a bad head it must be, to forget that Madam Yarico prevented her countrymen from peeling off the upper part of it. (*Aside.*) [*Exit.*

Inkle. 'Sdeath, what am I about? How have I slumbered? "Rouse, rouse, good Thomas Inkle!" Is it I---. I---who, in London, laugh'd at the younkers of the town ---and when I saw their chariots, with some fine, tempting girl, perk'd in the corner, come shopping to the city, wou'd cry---Ah!---there sits ruin--there flies the Greenhorn's money! then wonder'd with myself how men cou'd trifle time on women; or, indeed, think of any women without fortunes. And now, forsooth, it rests with *me* to turn romantic puppy, and give up All for Love.--- Give up!---Oh monstrous folly---thirty thousand pounds'!

Trudge.

Trudge.   (*Peeping in at the door.*)

Trudge. May I come in, Sir?
Inkle. What does the booby want?
Truage. Sir, your uncle wants to fee *you.*
Inkle. Mr. Medium! Shew him up directly.

[*Exit* Trudge.

He muft not know of this.——To-morrow!——"I muft
" be blunt with Yarico." I wifh this marriage were
more diftant, that I might break it by degrees: She'd
take my purpofe better, were it lefs fuddenly deliver'd.
" Womens weak minds bear grief as colts do burdens:
" Load them with their full weight at once, and they
" fink under it; but, every day, add little imperceptibly,
" to little, 'tis wonderful how much they'll carry."

Enter Medium.

Med. Ah! here he is! Give me your hand, Nephew!
welcome, welcome to Barbadoes, with all my heart.
Inkle. I am glad to meet you here, Unkle!
Med. That you are, that you are, I'm fure; Lord!
Lord! when we parted laft, how I wifh'd we were in
a room together, if it was but the black hole! " Since
we funder'd," I have not been able to fleep o'nights, for
thinking of you. I've laid awake, and fancied I faw you
fleeping your laft, with your head in a lion's mouth, for
a night cap; and I've never feen a bear brought over,
to dance about the ftreet, but I thought you might be
bobbing up and down in its belly.
Inkle. I am very much oblig'd to you.
Med. Ay, ay, I am happy enough to find you fafe
and found, I promife you. " Why, I've been hunting
" you all over the quay, and been in half the houfes upon
" it, before I cou'd find you; I fhould have been here foon-
" er elfe. Whew!---I'm fo warm---I've run as faft——
" *Inkle.* As you did in the foreft---Eh! Mr. Me-
"dium?
" *Med.* Well, well; thank heaven we are both
" out of the foreft! Hounflow-heath at dufk is a trifle

" to

" to it. I shall never see a tree without shaking; and,
" I cou'd not walk in a grove again with comfort; tho'
" it were in the middle of Paradise." But, you have a
fine prospect before you now, young man. I am come
to take you with me to Sir Christopher, who is impatient to see you.

Inkle. To-morrow, I hear, he expects me.

Med. To-morrow! directly----this moment----in
half a second.----I left him standing on tip-toe, as he
calls it, to embrace you; and he's standing on tip-toe
now in the great parlour, and there he'll stand till you
come to him.

Inkle. Is he so hasty?

Med. Hasty! he's all pepper---and wonders you are
not with him, before it's possible to get at him. Hasty
indeed! Why he vows you shall have his daughter this
very night.

Inkle. What a situation!

Med. Why, it's hardly fair just after a voyage.
But come, bustle, bustle, he'll think you neglect him.
He's rare and touchy, I can tell you; and if he once
takes it into his head that you shew the least slight to
his daughter, it wou'd knock up all your schemes in a
minute.

Inkle. Confusion! If he should hear of Yarico! *(Aside.)*

Med. But at present you are all and all with him; he
has been telling me his intentions these six weeks; you'll
be a fine warm husband, I promise you.

Inkle. This cursed connection! *(Aside.)*

Med. It is not for me though to tell you how to play
your cards; you are a prudent young man, and can
make calculations in a wood. "I need not tell you
" that the least shadow of affront disobliges a testy old
" fellow: but, remember, I never speak ill of my friends."

Inkle. Fool! fool! fool! *(Aside.)*

Med. Why, what the devil is the matter with you?

Inkle. It must be done effectually, or all is lost; mere
parting would not conceal it. *(Aside.)*

Med. Ah! now he's got to his damn'd Square Root
again, I suppose, and Old Nick would not move him---
Why, nephew!

Inkle,

Inkle. The planter that I fpoke with cannot be arriv'd---but time is precious---the firft I meet---com-
mon prudence now demands it. I'm fix'd; I'll part
with her. (*Afide.*)　　　　　　　　　　　[*Exit.*

Med. Damn me, but he's mad! The woods have
turn'd the poor boy's brains; he's fcalp'd, and gone
crazy! Holo! Inkle! Nephew! Gad, I'll fpoil your
arithmetick, I warrant me.　　　　　　　　[*Exit.*

S C E N E, *The Quay.*

Enter Sir Chriftopher Curry

Sir Chr. Ods my life! I can fcarce contain my happinefs. I have left e'm fafe in church in the middle of the
ceremony. I ought to have given Narciffa away, they
told me; but I caper'd about fo much for joy, that Old
Spintext advifed me to go and cool my heels on the quay,
till it was all over. Odd, I'm fo happy! and they fhall
fee, now, what an old fellow can do at a wedding.

Enter Inkle.

Inkle. Now for difpatch! Hark'ee, old gentleman!
(*to the governor*).

Sir Chr. Well, young gentleman?

Inkle. If I miftake not, I know your bufinefs here.

Sir Chr. 'Egad, I believe half the ifland knows it, by
this time.

Inkle. Then to the point---I have a female, whom I
wifh to part with.

Sir Chr. Very likely; it's a common cafe, now a-
days, with many a man.

Inkle. If you could fatisfy me you would ufe her
mildly, and treat her with more kindnefs than is ufual---
for I can tell you fhe's of no common ftamp---perhaps
we might agree.

Sir Chr. Oho! a flave! Faith, now I think on't, my
daughter may want an attendant or two extraordinary;
　　　　　　　　　　　　　　　　　　　　　　and

and as you say she's a delicate girl, above the common run, and none of your thick-lip'd, flat-nos'd, squabby, dumpling dowdies, I don't much care if---

Inkle. And for her treatment---

Sir Chr. Look ye, young man; I love to be plain: I shall treat her a good deal better than you wou'd, I fancy; for, though I witness this custom every day, I can't help thinking the only excuse for buying our fellow creatures, is to rescue 'em from the hands of those who are unfeeling enough to bring them to market.

Inkle. "Somewhat too blunt, Sir; I am no common trafficker, dependent upon proud rich planters." Fair words, old gentleman; an Englishman won't put up an affront.

Sir Chr. An Englishman! More shame for you! "Let Englishmen blush at such practices." Men, who so fully feel the blessings of liberty, are doubly cruel in depriving the helpless of their freedom.

" *Inkle.* Confusion!

" *Sir Chr.* 'Tis not my place to say so much; but I can't help speaking my mind.

Inkle. "I must be cool"---Let me assure you, Sir, 'tis not my occupation; but for a private reason---an instant pressing necessity---

Sir Chr. Well, well, I have a pressing necessity, too; I can't stand to talk now; I expect company here presently; but if you'll ask for me to-morrow, at the Castle--

Inkle. The Castle!

Sir Chr. Aye, Sir, the Castle; the Governor's Castle; known all over Barbadoes.

Inkle. 'Sdeath, this man must be on the Governor's establishment: his steward, perhaps, and sent after me, while Sir Christopher is impatiently waiting for me. I've gone too far; my secret may be known---As 'tis, I'll win this fellow to my interest. (*to him*) One word more, Sir: my business must be done immediately; and as you seem acquainted at the Castle, if you should see me there---and there I mean to sleep to-night---

Sir Chr. The Devil you do!

Inkle. Your finger on your lips; and never breath a fyll: e of this tranfaction.

Sir Chr. No! Why not?

Inkle. Becaufe, for reafons, which perhaps you'll know to-morrow, I might be injured with the Governor, whofe moft particular friend I am.

Sir Chr. So here's a particular friend of mine, coming to fleep at my houfe, that I never faw in my life. I'll found this fellow. (*Afide.*) I fancy, young gentleman, as you are fuch a bofom friend of the Governor's, you can hardly do any thing to alter your fituation with him? " I " fhou'dn't imagine any thing could bring him to think " a bit worfe of you than he does at prefent."

Inkle. Oh! pardon me; but you'll find that hereafter-- befides you, doubtlefs know his character?

Sir Chr. Oh, as well as I do my own. But let's underftand one another. You may truft me, now you've gone fo far. You are acquainted with his character, no doubt to a hair?

Inkle. I am---I fee we fhall underftand each other. You know him too, I fee, as well as I.---A very touchy, tefty, hot old fellow.

Sir Chr. Here's a fcoundrel! I hot and touchy! Zounds! I can hardly contain my paffion!---But I won't difcover myfelf. I'll fee the bottom of this--- (*to him*). Well now, as we feem to have come to a tolerable explanation---Let's proceed to bufinefs---Bring me the woman.

Inkle. No; there you muft excufe me. I rather wou'd avoid feeing her any more; and wifh it to be fettled without my feeming interference. My prefence might diftrefs her.---You conceive me?

Sir Chr. Zounds! what an unfeeling rafcal!---The poor girl's in love with him, I fuppofe. No, no, fair and open. My dealing's with you, and you only: I fee her now, or I declare off.

Inkle. Well then, you muft be fatisfied: yonder's my fervant--ha--a thought has ftruck me.---Come here, Sir.

3   *Enter*

Enter Trudge.

I'll write my purpofe, and fend it her by him.—It's lucky that I taught her to decypher characters; my labour now is paid." (*Takes out his pocket-book and writes.*) —This is fomewhat lefs abrupt; 'twill foften matters (*to himfelf*). Give this to Yarico; then bring her hither with you.

Trudge. I fhall, Sir. (*Going.*)

Inkle. Stay; come back. This foft fool, if uninftructed, may add to her diftrefs: his drivelling fympathy may feed her grief, inftead of foothing it.—When fhe has read this paper, feem to make light of it; tell her it is a thing of courfe, done purely for her good. I here inform her that I muft part with her. D'ye underftand your leffon?

Trudge. Pa—part with Ma—madam Ya-ric-o!

Inkle. Why does the blockhead ftammer!—I have my reafons. No muttering—And let me tell you, Sir, if your rare bargain were gone too, 'twou'd be the better: fhe may babble our ftory of the foreft, and fpoil my fortune.

Trudge. I'm forry for it, Sir; I have lived with you a long while; I've half a year's wages too due the 25th *ulto.* due for dreffing your hair, and fcribbling your parchments; but take my fcribbling; take my frizzing; take my wages; and I, and Wows, will take ourfelves off together—fhe fav'd my life, and rot me, Sir, if any thing but death fhall part us.

Inkle. Impertinent! Go, and deliver your meffage.

Trudge. I'm gone, Sir. Lord, Lord! I never carried a letter with fuch ill will in all my born days. [*Exit.*

Sir Chr. Well—fhall I fee the girl?

Inkle. She'll be here prefently. One thing I had forgot: when fhe is your's, I need not caution you, after the hints I've given, to keep her from the caftle. If Sir Chriftopher fhould fee her, 'twould lead, you know, to a difcovery of what I wifh conceal'd.

Sir Chr. Depend upon me—Sir Chriftopher will

I   know

know no more of our meeting, than he does at this moment.

Inkle. Your secrecy shall not be unrewarded: I'll recommend you, particularly, to his good graces.

Sir Chr. Thank ye, thank ye; but I'm pretty much in his good graces, as it is; I don't know any body he has a greater respect for.——

Re-enter Trudge.

Inkle. Now, Sir, have you perform'd your message?

Trudge. Yes, I gave her the letter.

Inkle. And where is Yarico? did she say she'd come? didn't you do as you were order'd? didn't you speak to her?

Trudge. I cou'dn't, Sir, I cou'dn't---I intended to say what you bid me---but I felt such a pain in my throat, I cou'dn't speak a word, for the soul of me; and so, Sir, I fell a crying.

Inkle. Blockhead!

Sir Chr. 'Sblood, but he's a very honest blockhead. Tell me, my good fellow---what said the wench?

Trudge. Nothing at all, Sir. She sat down with her two hands clasp'd on her knees, and look'd so pitifully in my face, I cou'd not stand it. Oh, here she comes. I'll go and find Wows. If I must be melancholy, she shall keep me company.

Sir Chr. Ods my life, as comely a wench, as ever I saw!

Enter Yarico, *who looks some time in* Inkle's *face, bursts into tears, and falls on his neck.*

Inkle. In tears! nay, Yarico! why this?

Yar. Oh do not---do not leave me!

Inkle. Why, simple girl! I'm labouring for your good. My interest, here, is nothing; I can do nothing from myself; you are ignorant of our country's customs. I

must

must give way to men more powerful, who will not have me with you. But see, my Yarico, ever anxious for your welfare, I've found a kind good person, who will protect you.

Yarico. Ah! why not you protect me!

Inkle. I have no means---how can I?

Yarico. Just as I shelter'd you. Take me to yonder mountain, where I see no smoke from tall, high houses, fill'd with your cruel countrymen. None of your princes, there, will come to take me from you: And, should they stray that way, we'll find a lurking place, just like my own poor cave; where many a day. I sat beside you, and bless'd the chance that brought you to it---that I might save your life.

Sir Chr. His life! Zounds! my blood boils at the scoundrel's ingratitude!

Yar. Come, come, let's go. I always fear'd these cities. Let's fly and seek the woods; and there we'll wander hand in hand together. No cares shall vex us then---We'll let the day glide by in idleness; and you shall sit in the shade, and watch the sun-beam playing on the brook; while I will sing the song that pleases you. No cares, love, but for food---and we'll live cheerily I warrant---In the fresh, early morning, you shall hunt down our game, and I will pick you berries---and then, at night, I'll trim our bed of leaves, and lie me down in peace---Oh! we shall be so happy!---

Inkle. " This is mere trifling---the trifling of an un- " enlighten'd Indian." Hear me, Yarico: My countrymen and your's differ as much in minds as in complexions. We were not born to live in woods and caves---to seek subsistence by pursuing beasts---We christians, girl, hunt money; a thing unknown to you--- But, here, 'tis money which brings us ease, plenty, command, power, every thing, and of course happiness. You are the bar to my attaining this; therefore 'tis necessary for my good---and which I think you value----

Yarico. You know I do; so much, that it wou'd break my heart to leave you.

I 2

Inkle.

Inkle. But we muſt part. If you are ſeen with me, I ſhall loſe all.

Yar. I gave up all for you---my friends---my country: all that was dear to me: and ſtill grown dearer ſince you ſhelter'd there---All, all was left for you---and were it now to do again---again I'd croſs the ſeas, and follow you all the world over.

Inkle. We idle time; Sir, ſhe is your's. See you obey this gentleman; 'twill be the better for you. *(going.)*

Yar. O barbarous! *(holding him)* Do not, do not abandon me!

Inkle. No more.

Yar. Stay but a little. I ſhan't live long to be a burden to you. Your cruelty has cut me to the heart. Protect me but a little---or I'll obey this man, and un-dergo all hardſhips for your good; ſtay but to witneſs 'em. I ſoon ſhall ſink with grief; tarry till then; and hear me bleſs your name when I am dying; and beg you, now and then, when I am gone, to heave a ſigh for your poor Yarico.

Inkle. I dare not liſten. You, Sir, I hope, will take good care of her. *(going.)*

Sir Chr. Care of her!---that I will---I'll cheriſh her like my own daughter; and pour balm into the heart, of a poor, innocent girl, that has been wounded by the artifices of a ſcoundrel.

Inkle. Hah! 'Sdeath, Sir, how dare you!---

Sir Chr. 'Sdeath, Sir, how dare you look an honeſt man in the face?

Inkle. Sir, you ſhall feel---

Sir Chr. Feel!---It's more than ever you did, I be-lieve. Mean, ſordid, wretch! dead to all ſenſe of honour, gratitude, or humanity---I never heard of ſuch barbarity! I have a ſon-in-law, who has been left in the ſame ſitu-ation; but, if I thought him capable of ſuch cruelty, dam'nie if I wou'd not turn him to ſea, with a peck loaf, in a cockle ſhell---Come, come, cheer up, my girl!

You

You fhan't want a friend to protect you, I warrant you.---(*taking* Yarico *by the hand.*)

Inkle. Infolence! The Governor fhall hear of this infult.

Sir Chr. The Governor! lyar! cheat! rogue! impoftor! breaking all ties you ought to keep, and pretending to thofe you have no right to. The Governor had never fuch a fellow in the whole catalogue of his acquaintance---the Governor difowns you---the Governor difclaims you---the Governor abhors you; and to your utter confufion, here ftands the Governor to tell you fo. Here ftands old Curry, who never talk'd to a rogue without telling him what he thought of him.

Inkle. Sir Chriftopher!---Loft and undone!

Med. (*Without.*) Holo! Young Multiplication! Zounds! I have been peeping in every cranny of the houfe. Why young Rule of Three! (*Enters from the Inn*) Oh, here you are at laft.---Ah, Sir Chriftopher! What are you there! too impatient, I fee, to wait at home. But here's one that will make you eafy, I fancy. (*Clapping* Inkle *on the fhoulder.*)

Sir Chr. How came you to know him?

Med. Ha! ha! Well that's curious enough too. So you have been talking, here, without finding out each other?

Sir Chr. No, no; I have found him out, with a vengeance.

Med. Not you. Why this is the dear boy. It's my nephew, that is; your fon-in-law, that is to be. It's Inkle!

Sir Chr. It's a lie; and you're a purblind, old booby--- and this dear boy is a damn'd fcoundrel.

Med. Hey-dey, what's the meaning of this? One was mad before, and he has bit the other, I fuppofe.

Sir Chr. But here comes the dear boy---the true boy---the jolly boy, piping hot from church, with my daughter.

Enter

Enter Campley, Narcissa, *and* Patty.

Med. Campley!

Sir Chr. Who? Campley?---It's no such thing.

Camp. That's my name, indeed, Sir Christopher.

Sir Chr. The Devil it is! And how came you, Sir,
to impose upon me, and assume the name of Inkle? A
name which every man of honesty ought to be ashamed
of.

Camp. I never did, Sir.—Since I sailed from England
with your daughter, my affection has daily encreased
and when I came to explain myself to you, by a number
of concurring circumstances, which I am now partly
acquainted with, you mistook me for that gentleman. Yet
had I even then been aware of your mistake, I must con-
fess, the regard for my own happiness would have tempted
me to let you remain undeceiv'd.

Sir Chr. And did you, Narcissa, join in—

Nar. How could I, my dear Sir, disobey you?

Patty. Lord, your honour, what young Lady could
refuse a Captain?

Camp. I am a Soldier, Sir Christopher. Love and
War, is the soldier's motto; and tho' my income is trifling to your *intended* son-in-law's, still the chance of war
has enabled me to support the object of my love above
indigence. Her fortune, Sir Christopher, I do not consider myself by any means entitled to.

Sir Chr. 'Sblood! but you must tho'. Give me your
hand, my young Mars, and bless you both together!
---Thank you, thank you for cheating an old fool into
giving his daughter to a lad of spirit, when he was going
to throw her away upon one in whose breast the mean
passion of avarice smothers the smallest spark of affection,
or humanity.

Inkle. Confusion!

Nar. I have this moment heard a story of a transac-
tion in the forest, which, I own, would have rendered a
compliance with your former commands very disagree-
able.

Patty.

Patty. Yes, Sir, I told my miſtreſs he had brought over a Hotty-pot gentlewoman.

Sir Chr. Yes, but he would have left her for you; (*To Narciſſa*) and you for his intereſt; and ſold you, perhaps, as he has this poor girl to me, as a requital for preſerving his life.

Nar. How!

Enter Trudge *and* Wowſki.

Trudge. Come along, Wows! take a long laſt leave of your poor Miſtreſs: throw your pretty, ebony arms about her neck.

Wows. No, no;---ſhe not go; you not leave poor Wowſki. (*Throwing her arms about* Yarico.)

Sir Chr. Poor girl! A companion I take it!

Trudge. A thing of my own, Sir. I cou'dn't help following my maſter's example in the woods---*Like Maſter, like Man.*

Sir Chr. But you wou'd not ſell her, and be hang'd to you, you dog, wou'd you?

Trudge. Hang me, like a dog, if I wou'd, Sir.

Sir Chr. So ſay I to every fellow that breaks an obligation due to the feelings of a man. But, old Medium, what have you to ſay for your hopeful nephew?

Med. I never ſpeak ill of my friends, Sir Chriſtopher.

Sir Chr. Pſhaw!

Inkle. Then let me ſpeak: hear me defend a conduct――――

Sir Chr. Defend! Zounds! plead guilty at once---- its the only hopes left of obtaining mercy.

Inkle. Suppoſe, old Gentleman, you had a ſon?

Sir Chr. S'blood! then I'd make him an honeſt fellow; and teach him, that the feeling heart never knows greater pride than when it's employ'd in giving ſuccour to the unfortunate. I'd teach him to be his father's own ſon to a hair.

Inkle. Even ſo my father tutor'd me: from infancy, bending my tender mind like a young ſapling, to his

will

will---Intereſt was the grand prop round which he twin'd
my pliant, green affections: taught me in childhood to
repeat old ſayings--all tending to his own fix'd principles--
and the firſt ſentence that I ever liſp'd, was *Charity begins
at Home.*

Sir Chr. I ſhall never like a proverb again as long as
I live.

Inkle. As I grew up, he'd prove---and by example
---were I in want, I might e'en ſtarve, for what the
world cared for their neighbours; why then ſhou'd I care
for the world? Men now liv'd for themſelves. Theſe
were his doctrines: then, Sir, what wou'd you ſay,
ſhould I, in ſpite of habit, precept, education, fly in my
father's face, and ſpurn his councils?

Sir Chr. Say! why, that you were a damn'd honeſt,
undutiful fellow. O curſe ſuch principles! Principles,
which deſtroy all confidence between man and man---
Principles, which none but a rogue cou'd inſtil, and
none but a rogue cou'd imbibe.---Principles----

Inkle. Which I renounce.

Sir Chr. Eh!

Inkle. Renounce entirely. Ill-founded precept too
long has ſteel'd my breaſt---but ſtill 'tis vulnerable---
this trial was too much--Nature, 'gainſt Habit combating
within me, has penetrated to my heart; a heart, I own,
long callous to the feelings of ſenſibility; but now it
bleeds---and bleeds for my poor Yarico. Oh, let me
claſp her to it, while 'tis glowing, and mingle tears of
love and penitence. *[Embracing her.]*

Trudge. *[Capering about.]* Wows give me a kiſs!
[Wows goes to Trudge.

Yar. And ſhall we--ſhall we be happy?

Inkle. Aye; ever, ever, Yarico.

Yarico. I knew we ſhou'd---and yet I fear'd---but
ſhall I ſtill watch over you? Oh, Love, you, ſurely,
gave your Yarico ſuch pain, only to make her feel this
happineſs the greater.

Wows. *(Going to Yarico)* Oh Wowſki ſo happy!---
and yet I think I not glad neither.

Trudge. Eh, Wows! How!---why not?

Wows.

Wows. 'Caufe I can't help cry.————

Sir Chr. Then, if that's the cafe————curfe me, if I think I'm very glad either. What the plague's the matter with my eyes?---Young man, your hand---I am now proud and happy to fhake it.

Med. Well, Sir Chriftopher, what do you fay to my hopeful nephew now?

Sir Chr. Say! Why, confound the fellow, I fay, that is ungenerous enough to remember the bad action of a man, who has virtue left in him to repent it.———— As for you, my good fellow, (*to* Trudge) I muft, with your mafter's permiffion, employ you myfelf.

Trudge. O rare!----blefs your honour!---Wows! you'll be Lady, you jade, to a Governor's Factotum.

Wows. Iis---I Lady Jacktotum.

Sir Chr. And now, my young folks, we'll drive home, and celebrate the wedding! Od's my life! I long to be fhaking a foot at the fiddles: and I fhall dance ten times the lighter, for reforming an Inkle, while I have it in my power to reward the innocence of a Yarico.

F I N A L E.

C A M P L E Y.

Come let us dance and fing,
While all Barbadoes bells fhall ring :
Love fcrapes the fiddle-ftring,
*　And Venus plays the lute ;*
Hymen gay, foots away,
Happy at our wedding-day,
Cocks his chin, and figures in,
*　To tabor, fife, and flute.*

C H O R U S.

Come then dance and fing,
While all Barbadoes bells fhall ring, &c.

K　　　　　　CHORUS,

NARCISSA.

Since, thus, each anxious care
Is vanish'd into empty air,
Ah! how can I forbear
    To join the jocund dance?
To and fro, couples go,
On the light fantastic toe,
While with glee, merrily,
    The rosy hours advance.   Chorus.

YARICO.

When first the swelling sea
Hither bore my love and me,
What then my fate would be,
    Little did I think---
Doom'd to know care and woe,
Happy still is Yarico;
Since her love will constant prove,
    And nobly scorns to shrink.

TRUDGE.

'Sbobs! now I'm fix'd for life,
My fortune's fair, tho' black's my wife,
Who fears domestic strife---
    Who cares now a souse!
Merry cheer my dingy dear
Shall find, with her Factotum here;
Night and day, I'll frisk and play,
    About the house, with Wows.   Chorus.

PATTY.

A N   O P E R A.

P A T T Y.

last word (handwritten)

Let Patty say a word———
A chambermaid may sure be heard———
Sure men are grown absurd,
  Thus taking black for white!
To hug and kiss a dingy miss,
Will hardly suit an age like this———
Unless, here, some friends appear,
  Who like this wedding night.   Chorus,

T H E   E N D.

CPSIA information can be obtained
at www.ICGtesting.com
Printed in the USA
BVHW051627261118
534009BV00033B/2376/P

9 780243 460588